ON THE FRINGE
OF A CLOUD

By

Carensa Lily Harris

CONTENTS

ACKNOWLEDGMENTS

I would love to give a special thank you to my Bampa for helping with the corrections in this book.

CHAPTER 1

I was being chased – but by what? I was galloping like a horse through the forest, as fast as my little legs could go. The forest was creepy, dark and gloomy – nothing as haunted as my eyes have ever seen before. It was a cold night so I was able to see my breath spill from my lungs.

As soon as I looked away from the forest floor, I tripped over a tree root that was just edging out of the ground. As I landed, there was a powerful wave of silence that rippled throughout the forest. As I gazed around, all I could hear was my heart beating, I was scared. I was petrified, I didn't know what would happen next. Then it came, looming out of the shadows, it had its bloodthirsty eyes and its knife-like claws ready to eat me, and... that's when I woke up from my dream!

As my heart rate slowed down, I stretched and yawned while opening my eyes to adjust to the morning light. I walked sleepily over to my bathroom, with my feet rubbing the soft and fluffy rug, to wash my face and brush my teeth. Then I wandered down my winding, wooden stairs (which were amazingly not creaky this morning) to soothe my rumbling stomach with some waffles, Nutella and strawberries. It was delicious!

Before I proceed, my name is Nova Heck! I have an older sister who's adopted and works in the navy with a name of Jasmine, with ginger hair and hazel eyes. Then I have a mother who is extremely protective over me. Her name is Jane and she has light brown hair with soft hazel eyes and a long nose. And a dad who I see once a year because he is a photographer that travels the world; he has brown hair, crystal-blue eyes and freckles like me. His name is Jaimie! So, it was just Jane and myself, but since it's the start of the summer holidays with the summer sun, the clear sky, with bees and wasps pollinating our flowers, Mum decided to take me to Australia to see my other family members who live in Sydney! So that's where we are travelling tomorrow.

Anyways, today on this stunning, sunny morning Jane took me to McCarther Glen by bus (so we didn't have to park). McCarther Glen is a shopping centre, with many clothes and scrumptious food; you can definitely call me a foodie.

As we arrived, we instantly made our way to the Food Hall, but of course Jane had to bump into an old friend. Their reactions made it seem like they hadn't seen each other in years, they started screeching as the saw each other, this made me so embarrassed because it made a visible scene in front of all the shoppers. The shoppers must've thought that somebody had found out terrible news.

Jane gave me a heads up before she started talking, "Only five minutes, darling, then we can get some food!" but they chatted like there was no tomorrow. Well it was twenty minutes later, and I heard the gurgling of my stomach start. It was like my stomach was a volcano about to erupt.

I gave Mum the 'I'm HUNGRY stare', then she knew it was time to get food. So, she gave her friend Sarah a loose hug and spoke, "I have got to go, have a lovely summer."

Sarah replied, "I haven't got your number!"

I instantly thought to myself, *Here goes another twenty minutes of my life*. But I was surprised, it only took five. As time went on, we went to the Food Hall about twenty-five minutes later than we had planned; we ordered hot noodles with oyster chicken (Jane had a side of black bean sauce, I kept it out).

Afterwards, I scraped the chicken out from between my teeth and gathered my things to go all over the shopping centre, in search of summer clothes!

As I went to my first dress shop, Jane obviously found her other friend, but this time from work. So that was another hour gone out of the window. I decided to make life easier for myself and interrupted their "forever lasting" conversation, and spoke in a courteous manner. "Sorry but, I'm just going to go shopping, do you mind if I leave this shop and buy some clothes? While you ladies talk," I asked with a smile on my face, crossing my fingers behind my back.

"Yes of course, my darling, I will be with you in a sec, you go," she replied with happy squinty eyes. When Jane says "...be with you in a sec..." that probably means just around an hour and a half. So, I just went off shopping and came upon this magnificent dress not so long after. I was surprised because I have high standards, so to find a dress that quick was a miracle, but I might have spoken too soon. It was all white with lace at the top and sparkly diamonds at the bottom, it was one of those dresses where the back is longer than the front and the legs are made to be very visible. But the thing was that the price was £235.99. My mum would freak if she knew I bought it. So, I just went with a casual dress, that had an ombre colour from yellow to orange. Which I thought was perfect, and less expensive so, win-win.

A couple hours had passed, and in the end, Jane did officially stop talking and did some shopping; we did quite well with the time we had.

Then it was time to go, so we caught the bus back home, the ride was awful.

As the bus stopped at our street the doors opened and a blast of fresh air filled our lungs. It was an extremely hot and sweaty bus filled with people; even my water bottle had turned warm.

I jumped in the cold and refreshing shower, which was such a great idea, only because I started having heat rashes in random places. Whilst downstairs, Jane was making her signature dish ready for tea; we only had it a few times a year, so you could tell Jane was in a terrific mood.

As time flew by, after drying my hair and choosing an outfit, I raced down the stairs at the smell of the sweet'n'savoury meal that was waiting for me, it was the smell of freshly made bread, sizzling steak and caramelised sweet potatoes. "Mmm!" I could just hear my stomach hum to itself. This was the life!

Mum and I had cookie dough for dessert (we were having a cheat day) while watching a romantic movie in my bedroom on my giant beanbags. I cried in parts with the boxes of tissues empty scattered on the floor, although of course it was romantic, which did make me feel lonely, but I was in no rush for love. Then as it got late, and the sky was wrapped in a grey blanket where the shining stars were out, we made our way to bed ready for the next morning.

CHAPTER 2

Extremely early the next day (when the sun wasn't even out, which to some people isn't a big deal, but to me normally waking up late, was) we were driven to the airport by taxi at 4:10am! We had to catch our plane in 3 hours, even though we only lived 5 minutes away; Jane always has this panic side of her and this is an example, because she always thinks we are going to miss the plane (by the way we never do because of her crazy timings that she makes me wake up at). While we were in the taxi, it was daunting (just like my dream). As we were driving through the narrow lanes, I thought something was going to jump out at the taxi from behind the bushes, this made me sink into my seat at shut my eyes tight.

Although it was 4:15am, our first thought was 'FOOD' because everything was happening so fast, as our first priority was to get to the airport. We went searching for a good 10 minutes and finally found a 1960s diner café, with the chequered floor (black and white), pink walls, waitresses on skates, an open kitchen, great atmosphere and happy people. Abruptly, we were served straight away by a young adult, with pink hair, just like Frankie's in the film 'Grease'. I ordered American pancakes with maple syrup, bacon, blueberries and icing sugar. But I asked for no icing sugar but more blueberries. Jane asked for the English breakfast, the biggest one on the menu (she eats a crazy amount when she is stressed) and to top it off we both had freshly squeezed orange juice. Surprisingly, it came straight away, considering the amount of people that were there, we were also surprised about the amount of people at this time in the morning. Well, I guess everyone has different schedules and plans.

Since we were in economy, we were boarding last, which made me mad because I wanted to get on the plane to see what it was like; I'm the type of person that gets excited over the interior of hotel rooms or restaurants and especially, aeroplane seats. It came up to 6:55am and we had still not boarded; you could tell what Jane was like because she believes that if you haven't boarded before the time that the plane was due to take off, then the plane will leave you, I don't know what goes on inside her head.

After a long wait, we could finally board. We strolled onto the plane with our light backpacks and sat 3 rows from the front, not too far from the toilets (thank goodness they did not smell). Jane had the aisle seat and I was placed in the middle.

As we took off at 7:20am (which was not bad for a delay of 5 minutes) I felt like a baby bird, flying for the first time out of the nest, swooping in the sky feeling free, I felt like I was in an action movie, going at the speed of light, it gave me exhilarating chills. But my mum had a completely different experience.

Jane gripped my hand very tight; adding on to her stress of being late, she could not stand flying in aeroplanes, she hated it; I remember when she told me what it felt like for her when we were safe and allowed our belts off.

She said, "I've had bad experiences on planes, remember when we almost crashed and died!" She was probably overexaggerating on the 'died' part, but she carried on while gripping my hand even harder.

"…I just feel that we are going to have turbulence and crash, I'm going to be sick!" She tore her seat belt off and ran to the toilets a few rows down. Luckily, she had an aisle seat, so it didn't turn into chaos! The flight attendant followed after her worriedly. I was grossed out at that moment and you probably are as well, so I decided to go to put on a comedy film, to help it get out of my head. I watched 'Daddy's Home' – it was very hilarious and got the memory out of my head as soon as I started laughing which was very early into the film. You can always count on comedy.

An hour passed and Jane came back looking like a green goblin with the attendant holding her up. Our flight attendant's name was Clarissa. She was very kind and would do anything for us, for even considering how hard we were to deal with (*cough, 'Jane being a drama queen', cough*), she wanted us to have the best time on this flight and to book again (that's how much she loved her job).

However, after our 10-minute chat about 'her life' (which by the way sounded amazing), I ordered 'Hoisin Duck, soy sauce, thin pancakes, spring onions and cucumber'.

Jane ordered 'Salmon, noodles and soy sauce'. It came pretty quick, but let me tell you as it came, it filled the plane with a homey scent and at the same time it looked very posh; it seemed that they had put time into our dishes. As we dug in, we turned our TVs on and I watched 'High School Musical' and Jane watched 'Midsomer Murders'. It was a series.

The atmosphere was amazingly happy after 11 hours on the plane; there were no babies crying and no angry parents, so all was good. We only had half an hour left so I had a miniature snooze with Mum. Clarissa was kind enough to bring around their special brand blankets and cushions. They were both so cosy, even when I was desperate for the toilet it was a struggle because it was so comfy.

As we descended from the sky, we had turbulence from the weather shaking our plane which, well you could say woke us all up (which made my heart rate increase and Jane almost have a panic attack). But we landed safe and sound, with a little bump on the runway, and Jane was very relieved judging by the way she let go of the arm rest from her tight grip.

CHAPTER 3

Our family member, Joey, who is my uncle and Jane's brother, picked us up from the airport and took us to his little cottage next to the stunning beach! I'm not even joking. The beach was something out of a movie.

We got there at 1am and everyone was asleep, so we just tip-toed over to the guest bedroom to catch some hours that were left to re-energise.

At 1:15am, the whole household woke at the sound of the loudest bang we had ever heard. Like a random gunshot. I sat upright in bed in a shot and reached dramatically for the lamp switch. As I sat up against the headboard, Jane was somehow still asleep.

"What on earth was that?" I whispered to myself. My heart rate was going like a drum in my chest. I had never felt nerves like this before. I shook Jane and she woke up moody.

"What time is it?" she moaned. She's not a morning person. In fact, I don't think anyone is at this time. But, when you hear something so terrifying, your body is so alert that you feel like it's the end for you, and you're never going to live another day.

"Are you serious? You're telling me that you didn't hear that sound?" I muttered viciously.

That's when it hit her. The look on her face, she was petrified. "Are you pranking me? If you are just leave me sleep, I'm tired and I don't want to be cranky in the morning!" She rolled back over. Her worriedness didn't last long.

I was so sure that I heard something. Maybe I was just jetlagged. Although, I always listen to my gut, even though I'm never right, I was certain about this.

I slid out of bed and wrapped my dressing gown around me, and walked out quietly, sneaking past Jane. But it didn't work. So, a sound like a gunshot wasn't loud enough but, my tippy-toe feet were. I seriously will never get her. Ever.

"Where are you going, Missy?" she squinted.

"Look, I one hundred percent, definitely heard something. I'm going to see what it was." I grabbed the door handle.

"Can't you wait until the morning? You might wake up everyone else," she tiredly argued.

"You don't think that the sound woke them up already? Just come with me." I tied my hair up as I was getting a little sweaty.

She rolled out of bed with attitude. "You better be right, if you aren't then you have to massage my feet tomorrow, I'm not even kidding." She looked at me with crazy hair.

We cautiously wandered into the lounge and found everyone awake with flashlights looking panicked.

The dad – John, the other brother of Jane who was my other uncle, went down to the basement, because that was where the THUD had come from. We all waited at the top of the crooked stairs, slowly following him down step-by-step. John told us, "Wait! I just heard a scrape, no-one move!"

Now I really felt like I was in a haunted movie where no-one comes out alive. Great. I couldn't have sweated more in my life.

The atmosphere was silent, you could hear fly wings buzzing on the other side of the room, you could hear people snoring in next door's house, you could even here the 'plink' of the water fall from the tap onto the metal surface of the sink, that was how tense and still the air was.

John did not like the feeling he was experiencing; he whispered, "I think we should go back to the lounge, sit down and have a cup of tea, while I ring the police."

We all agreed, I only agreed because 1: I am extremely lazy, 2: I wasn't in the mood to go ghost hunting tonight, and 3: I really fancied a warm cup of tea with a biscuit. I have never had a late-night craving this early. Weird.

The chilling part was that we could not see anything, the fuse box had been turned off, so no lights were working, and we couldn't turn it on because it was in the basement where the noise came from. Yes, we were scaredy cats. But tonight, was not the night to be brave. I also want to add that when we all made it to the lounge, we remembered that we couldn't even have teas as the electricity wasn't working. Just perfect.

As the police arrived at the haunted scene half an hour later, John and Rachel (who were married to each other), the parents of my cousins, showed the police to the basement and were trying to figure out what was happening.

Mum dragged me to the hallway where it wasn't so public and sounded stern (about the second part, anyway).

"OK, you were right, so you don't have to rub my feet tomorrow." I laughed. "But, I'm going to help, I can't just sit here."

"But who will protect me?"

"Look, now's not the time to be a baby, OK?" she shook me.

I looked at her all upset. "Mum, I'm scared though. What if you don't make it out? Who will I have?"

"Stop thinking like that! I will be perfectly fine. Now you stay with your cousins and try and fit in a nap if you can, I know what you can be like if you have no sleep."

"You think I can even close my eyes during this? Let alone have a nap."

"Just try. I will be quick, I promise. I love you." She kissed my forehead. Then I was left in the dark corridor. Well, not for long as I got goose bumps and ran into the lounge thinking something was behind me.

As I sat on the sofa surrounded by some of my family members, my nerves built up even more to the point that my stomach started to twist; without my mum I knew I was not safe.

So, I had to think of a way to follow Jane down to the basement. I don't know why I wanted to go so much because I was fine where I was, but I guess my nosiness just got the better of me. Maybe I didn't follow Jane to feel safe, maybe I just wanted to see it for myself. I thought that Aunt May wouldn't mind me going, so I just started strolling down the steps in plain sight, but she did mind and called me back.

"May, I have to go," I lied.

"No, you don't. Stay with us and we'll all get through this together," she sternly stated.

"I'm not afraid of what's down there. I guess I just want to see it for myself, maybe it'll teach me a lesson." I sat on the couch next to her.

"I said no." I fell onto my back with my arms out like a starfish and whined.

"Please," I patronised.

She sighed and didn't reply.

Then I thought, *You know what? It's my life, I can make the decisions. If I see something I don't like, then I'll have to live with it in my mind forever.* So I did the next craziest thing. I ran.

"Nova!" Aunt May tried to grab me, but her hip pain took her down.

"Sorry!" I yelled back.

At the bottom of the deep stairs, there was just a door. A very boring door, not much to say about it. The room was gloomy with a small light coming from the key lock. Like a door to heaven. I just stood there for a couple of moments seeing if I could catch a sound from the other room, almost like a sign telling me to turn back. But there was nothing. Not even a glimpse. It made me feel drawn into the mischievous wonders from behind.

I reached for the doorknob and creaked open the door with a flood of light washing the room. (Going back, I wish I hadn't opened the door at all.) I almost forgot to breathe as the horror image that stood before me took my normal function away. I dropped to the floor in fear. My heart missed a beat and I mean MISSED a beat. My eyes were fixated on Jane. My pupils grew smaller, and soon they burned from not blinking. I instantly cried. Shaking, trembling. I couldn't stand on my own two feet. I was fully dependent as I had lost the world to live.

"Mu... Mu... Mu..." I stumbled on my words.

My sight became misshapen as my tears tried to block out the terror. My own mother was paralysed. Laying on the floor, with her skin chalky white. Her fingertips light blue. She looked as if someone had drained the life out of her. That this was the end of the road for her. She was gone.

Rachel spotted me and darted over and hugged me tight. She didn't turn me around, so the hug was in the back of my mind.

"Nova," she weakly whispered. "I'm so sorry. She's gone."

That's the moment I couldn't move. That's the moment I ran out of breath. That's the moment I realised that the rest of my life I would be alone. That my best friend had left me.

"Mu... Mum?" I whispered. I grabbed Rachel's arm and held tight like a security blanket.

John yelled over, angry that I'd witnessed what had happened, "Rachel! Take her upstairs!" In these situations, you can't be angry at each other because there's more panic in the air than oxygen, so we know that John was only worried.

A soon as I heard John say this, I instantly wanted to see Jane. She felt so far away. "Please, Rachel. Let me see my mum. Please." I was getting weaker, and more desperate. This was torture for me. But so was it for Rachel.

"I'm sorry Nova. It's not safe. Let's go back upstairs and be with the cousins." I watched the police do what they could as Rachel was trying to lift me off the ground.

"H... how c...could you s...say that?" I stuttered badly.

She tried lifting me again, but I wasn't moving.

I started fighting, and she let me go instantly. With the admission to be free, I felt so much power in my legs that I ran so recklessly to Jane with no control. The moment my fingertip made contact with her wrist my body went into shock as my neck flung my head backwards; it felt like lightning bolts rippling throughout my bones, like a wave of ice drenching my body, the excruciating noise like church bells ringing in my ear. My lifeless body gave up and departed into a coma.

CHAPTER 4

I thought it would stop after the blackness. The bells kept ringing, the coldness made me frozen and the energy of the everlasting electricity retained its buzzing within my bones. I contemplated my surroundings, because all I could see was black. I was petrified that I would be stuck here, was this hell?

Then a blast of light knocked down the bare wall and I almost felt my body being dragged out. All I saw was the brightest buttery light, clouds beneath my feet. The pain was still there, but no longer did I feel it. I felt protected, like there was an imperceptible shield encompassing my body. All I felt was love, warmth and so inevitably powerfully good. I could hear wistful chirps from the birds, calming waves and the faintest of leaves fluttering in the gentle breeze. I was in paradise. I thought.

I didn't feel alive, that I had any control over my own body. I felt like a dream, but my gut knew it wasn't.

As I stared forwards, there was a very faint outline of a silhouette. I squinted, but it made no difference. I took a tiny step forward and the figure did too. I gathered a deep breath of fresh air and what was weird was that it felt so pure and clean as it flew gracefully through my respiratory system. Everything I did in this place always made it a thousand times better than when I was on Earth. Which kept me thinking, where was I?

I commenced my walk towards this figure and before I knew it, I was two feet away. It was a woman. She was a very beautiful woman and had flawless skin. She wore a weightless white dress with no shoes and had long ginger hair that had an effortless curl. As I gazed into her golden eyes, I saw power and goodness, I felt like she was reading my mind as she held out her hand next to my ear.

She spoke with grace, "Nova. My dearest. You are broken."

"Who are you?"

"I am God, Nova. Let me show you a special place." She gestured with her hands.

But I pulled back and had something to say. "What's the point of me living? Jane did everything for me so how can I know where to go or what to do?"

God confirmed, "Oh Nova. Your mother Jane is a strange one. But, she's just in a coma. Just like you. Don't be worried, all she had was a little shock. I took her pain away quickly, so she wasn't hurt enough to be killed."

I smiled so hard when she said this that my jaw hurt. God hesitated for a while and a few moments later asked a question. "Why do you think you are not worthy enough to be without Jane?"

I didn't really know what to say, I was put on the spot. "Um... It's just Jane did everything for me, so I'm dependant on her and my self-confidence is so low. I would just be so useless." She looked confused, so I looked confused.

She took a deep and I mean a DEEP breath before she put the story straight. "I created every single human being for a purpose. No matter how worthless they feel, or how pathetic, they have a reason to be there. Never hate yourself for not being perfect, I'm not perfect. Even though I make mistakes, none of them are humans," God promised. "Now, let's go to that place I talked about earlier."

She walked me over to a garden.

As we entered, it seemed very enchanted and peaceful and not one bad thought came to mind. We sat under a mossy green tree and stared at our gorgeous surroundings.

"Promise me something, Nova," as this angel crossed her legs.

"Anything." I was very calm.

"Make a difference. If you can, spread the message to the world. There are too many bad things happening, we need a change." Sometimes it was hard to listen because her angelic voice was so sentimental, you felt like a relaxed cloud, floating adrift into the abyss. But I heard what she said, and I would obey. I promised her and she said goodbye. "One last thing, Nova, you have the power to change the world, always remember that I'm right here next to you, I will protect you. I love you, Nova."

That was the last thing she said as all of my nearby views became blurred and my soul was falling from the sky. But, falling from heaven was much more relaxed than you would think.

Then before I knew it, I was laying safe and sound in the cloud-like hospital bed.

I opened my eyes and was surrounded by nurses glaring down at me with notepads and pens. I sat up in bed and all I could hear were gasps. Was this a good thing?

CHAPTER 5

"She's a miracle!" one nurse announced. I gazed at my heart rate on the computer screen and it was perfect. Everything was perfect.

"Are you feeling okay? You had a pretty bad shock." The nurse felt my forehead and checked the monitor.

"Yeah, I'm fine," I stuttered whilst being confused and holding my head like I had hit it. I thought to myself, *I was just in heaven and now I'm back on earth. My body is perfectly fine and apparently, I had a bad shock, but I didn't feel anything for long. Maybe I am a miracle and God was just protecting me.*

"How long have I been out for?" I was intrigued because it felt like five minutes.

"You've been passed out for two days straight." I could tell she was concerned. She held my hand and sat next to me on my bed as the other nurses exited the room. I was in so much shock at how long I was gone for, that the thought of it exhausted me, so I crashed my head on her shoulder. I just sat there for a couple of minutes in silence being grateful for being alive, whilst she rubbed my forehead. Soon after, there was a loud knock on the door. To me the loudness of the sound was déjà vu.

To my surprise it was a tall, worried doctor calling in desperate need for a nurse. "It's an emergency!" he yelled repeatedly, non-stop, running up and down the corridor knocking on everyone's door.

The only thing that he didn't realise (I mean when you're in a hurry and scared for someone's life I don't think you would check every door) was that apart from our room, every other room in this corridor was either a storage cupboard or a surgery room that was not in use. So, what I'm trying to sum up here is that he wasted his time, but you can't blame him really.

But before you ask, the nurse that was keeping me sane gave me a reassuring hug and sprinted out of the door to go help and to catch this apprehensive doctor. Then I was left, all by myself. I did have a few thoughts about leaving my room to go look for Jane, but with all these cords and tubes attached to me, I was frightened to get up and take them off in case I needed them.

So, I got comfy on my bed and gazed at the gorgeous pastel blue and pink balloons tied low at the end of my bed. As I looked closely, there was a shadow on the other side shaped like a rectangle on the table. I grabbed the rusty pair of crutches and tapped the balloons out of the way and as they pivoted around, there was a note. I love notes so I had to stand up and read it! Don't panic, I did not take any tubes or cords off my body, I just slowly rolled my personal machine over with me.

I gently flipped the note over in my hand and read the message.

Nova. I am OK, I just got hungry and the hospital food did not do it for me.
I'll be back soon! Hope you're OK.
Love you, Mum x

This made my stomach flip! (In a good way.) This was a sign of food. Good food. I did a little jump in the air (not to lose any cords) and swiftly walked back over to my bed and parked my body down. Now, I'm not the kind of person to fall asleep mid-day. I just can't do it, once it's bright and I'm fully awake, I can't go back to sleep. Therefore, I'm a terrible sleeper. But, somehow (I think it was the medication that made me feel drowsy) I fell asleep as soon as my head touched the pillow, literally.

Moments after, I only woke up because I had company. As soon as my ears caught the sound of the door squeak, I was up! I looked around and then realising that I couldn't see anything because I was facing the wall, I pivoted my head to see Jane. I'm not being selfish, but my stomach was mega excited to see a bag of food. My stomach definitely takes over my whole body, that's why I love food.

I sat up and got attacked by Jane's huge arms coming in for a hug.

"Baby I have missed you. I was out for a day and a half, but you were out for two days. Why did you come down the stairs, Nova? Why didn't you listen? The nurses kept saying that you wouldn't come back because of the force of the shock, I was so scared for you," she uttered, squeezing me tighter.

"OK, be careful with the tubes! Anyway, I love you way too much and you know that! I would always follow to make sure that you were safe, and you can't change that about me. Anyway, I am extremely nosy, so I just wanted to see what had happened," I elaborated. She let go of me and placed her hands on my face whilst viewing my eyes.

"I love you so much, but next time don't let your nosiness put your life on the line." She became serious.

After a couple of seconds of silence, I thought it was the best time to tell her about my experience with God. "Mum?" I quietly whispered.

"Yeah baby, what is it?" She placed the food bag down.

"Don't question me about this, I know what I saw, and I know what I heard." I became serious.

"What?" she raised her eyebrows.

"I met God. I went to heaven and we had an actual conversation."

"Baby, you didn't see anything. It was the drugs."

"THEN HOW AM I STILL ALIVE?!" I yelled, getting frustrated, I knew she wouldn't believe me.

"Shh, stop yelling. You're alive from the medication. You were most likely hallucinating. You didn't meet anyone." She was so stupid; I just became so annoyed with her and her ridiculous suggestions always making me feel less than her.

I ripped the cords and wires off my body, not giving a care in the world if they were important. "DON'T FOLLOW ME!" I shouted back before I left the room and ran down the corridor; she shot up from the bed and ran to the door frame and panicked running back to the bed, pressing the 'Emergency button' for a doctor to make sure I was safe.

I ran to reception and out into the humongous courtyard where many patients were. I walked out; out of breath with a red face I sat on a bench and looked up to the sky.

"Why? It felt so real, it has to be true!" I whispered.

A tear ran down my face, I had so much anger inside, but I had to let it go. If my experience wasn't a hallucination then I needed a sign, so I left it until I had a clear message. I couldn't be mad at Jane because we almost lost each other. I strode back inside with a smile on my face pretending to be OK. Then I saw Jane worried as ever, running down the corridor towards me with a doctor following.

"Nova. Stop doing this to me, I love you, what don't you understand about that? That's a hint that I don't want to lose you. OK? Do you understand?" She grabbed my arm.

I did feel a bit lightheaded which led to me collapsing after saying sassily, "I'm fine." I think I did too much exercise too quickly and I guess in the end I did need the tubes and cords. But nothing happened, I just slept with no further experience, which did disappoint.

When I woke up, Jane was sleeping in the chair next to me. I grabbed my crutches and tapped her on the knee. She woke instantly, worried, again. I gave her a huge hug and apologised, eating some more unhealthy food; it was kind of awkward after our argument but, we just kept eating. I did want to finish this conversation when we got home, but I turned into a happy person by the time we got there, and I wasn't in the mood for any more anger.

We were happily greeted by our family and went to get some rest for the next busy days of our travel. Jane slept right next to me and held me tight all throughout the night, not allowing me to move which was quite restricting. But I was very appreciative of her love.

CHAPTER 6

As the sun rose over the horizon, and the light soared through the thin curtain that draped over the square window, my eyes squinted and a yawn escaped from my mouth. May knocked on the door and brought in a smoothie bowl for me to eat in bed, but I slowly rolled out of bed and went into the lounge with her to discuss and clear up what just happened, leaving Jane in the bed to rest. First things first, I was eager to know how I became electrocuted from coming into contact with Mum.

"How did this happen? It makes no sense, why was I affected?" I said, feeling intrigued.

"Well, as Jane went downstairs to help out with the investigation, she didn't know that they had an 'electric fence' everywhere." I later found out that they were lending it to a farm down the road and I never found out why the fence was turned on, I mean what did they need it for? "So, as she spotted the figure hiding behind the worktable, Jane sprinted forward to catch him..." She hesitated with a crackly voice, "Then, um... she tripped on a brick," they were getting work done, "...and her neck landed on the electric wire and slit through her skin, but it miraculously didn't reach anything too important and the paramedics were extremely fast with their actions to stop her from bleeding to death. As you could've guessed the fence was alive and ready to zap anything to touch it. The paramedics didn't touch her with bare skin, they had thick gloves, but you weren't prepared for it and it almost killed you." Her eyes bawled with tears and she hugged me so tight. "Anyway, we also found out that the man hiding from the police in our basement was a robber from the bank a couple of miles away, he apparently held the taxi driver hostage in the car and chose any random house to hide in." Us talking woke up Jane for her to walk into the room and join in with the hug. I didn't know what to say, but I was extremely grateful to still be here.

Jane added, "You have been through all of this, and you have kept on going. If I was you, I would have broken down straight away and given up on life, but you inspire me so much, you are my sunshine when days are grey." I was imagining life without Jane; I couldn't do it. I reached over and gave her another cuddle. May smiled and rubbed my back and then walked out to make Jane's breakfast. Just to say, everyone else was still in bed.

"I couldn't have done it without you, Mum. I love you so much." We sat there for a while taking in every moment because at any time this could all be taken away from me.

Since this was our last night in Australia (I know, a very short holiday. We cut it short due to the event that took place.) my family suggested going for a walk on the beach. Now I understood why. It was magical, with the crystal-like sea glimmering in the moonlight. How could this get any better? There was even a lush restaurant at the other end of the beach so we could have food.

We had a couple of hours out and then my cousins and I had a race back home; I fell over a few times in ditches people had made in the sand and Julia always helped me out.

Then as we reached home, back from our eventful evening, I stayed outside as my relatives wandered back to bed. I rested on the deck chair in sight of the star-filled sky, I had some peaceful moments just staring at the sky with no thoughts. I could never imagine a life better than this. I had a perfect family, just enough money to live on and a beautiful location to travel to every single year for holidays. I winked at the sky, sent a smile because I now knew something was behind it. I thought I would give it a message that I was happy.

I whispered to the stars, "Now I'm back, it's time for a change. For everyone."

A couple, or even a couple more hours later, I woke up and I was in a mess. There was dribble everywhere (it started to crust on my lips), my hair was literally glued to my face. So, I gently tore the hair off my cheeks, whipped the duvet off my body and fell off my bed whacking my head on the hardwood side table, it hurt. Then I found my foot stuck in the bed sheet, you see how clumsy I am? Jane raced in from the room next door, which was the kitchen after hearing a bang.

"Ow, I need a little help," I whined, holding my hand in the air for assistance.

"Are you crazy or what? How on earth did this happen? It was only a few days ago you fell down the stairs after tripping over a hairbrush! You're lucky you haven't broken anything yet." Her expression demanded answers. But I didn't answer, we just laughed. "Right, breakfast is almost served. Rachel made pancakes." I jumped in the air with excitement!

As Jane left the room, I jumped in the shower, brushed my teeth, dried and braided my hair just in time for breakfast (I was very fast at braiding because I always practiced on Jane when I was bored).

Since their garden was literally on the beach, we sat in wooden deck chairs under their gigantic beach umbrella, that protected us from the blazing sun. My family had Nutella and banana crepes that looked amazing. While we scoffed our faces with these charming treats, I gazed out onto the clear sea and saw out of the corner of my eye a dark blur; I turned my head in the direction of the mysterious blur and it was a homeless couple that pleaded for money. Jane has always told me to stay away from these type of people, I never knew why. Jane saw me looking at the homeless couple and tried to distract me.

"Honey, are you enjoying your meal? It looks to me you are; you've got it all over your face!" as she wiped chocolate off my dirty chin, laughing.

"I am enjoying it, it's just that there is a homeless couple over by the rocks. I want to help!" Everyone stopped and gazed at Jane with a worried look, because they also knew Jane disliked those people. Rachel even lost grip of her fork and it bounced off her paper plate and straight into the golden sand and stood up by itself. As I stared at everyone's faces, I looked sharply at Jane and Jane looked at me in a way which said, 'Are you serious? You know I hate homeless people.' I hated that stare; you could even call it the death stare! If looks could kill, I would have... you know. Anyway, I just ignored Jane and sorted it out by myself. As my family went indoors, I had a mission to complete, this was my first task, and my first baby step to changing the world.

There was a nearby shop for me to buy some gifts. I put in the hamper fresh oranges, bananas, biscuits, four bottles of water, an umbrella, a thin woollen blanket, pants and socks, and lastly, a $50 note to let them buy more food, or whatever.

I packed the hamper with the items, with a big purple bow on the top! (I also got these from the shop and made the whole package there, out of sight of Jane.)

I then crept over to the homeless couple and announced proudly, "Hi, I'm Nova. I saw you needed some food so, I hope this hamper will do you good!" I placed it down in front of their shocked faces with my fingers crossed behind my back that Jane wouldn't see me.

"Oh my. You are so kind. What's in here?" I plopped on the floor and reached out to help open the hamper, undoing all of my hard work.

"Well, firstly, we have food. I saw you siting by the sea with a couple of coppers in your tiny crisp packet, you looked starving! So, I brought over fresh oranges, bananas and biscuits. To keep you dry and warm, I got an umbrella, a blanket and some pants and socks. For the extras I brought $50, for you to spend at any shop for clothes or food!" Their amazed faces warmed my heart, I love it when I make people happy.

"Thank you so much, darling, you are the sweetest and best thing that has ever happened to us. May I have a hug? It's the least we could do."

I smiled when leaning over into her open arms. As I went with the flow, I literally zoomed off Earth, remembering the time when I looked into God's eyes, seeing her power and goodness. Then suddenly, I heard a yell that sounded like my mother. I quickly zoomed back down to Earth. I said my goodbyes and stood up hurriedly.

"I have got to go now. I will never see you again, so I hope this hamper will do you well, for a long time. Bye!" Saying it while trying to skip happily away having adrenaline start to kick in. As soon as I was out of their sight, my smile turned upside down.

I could hear rummaging through the hamper once more. I could hear the package of biscuits being opened, I smiled in my head but outside, I was a nervous wreck to tell my mum where I had been.

She caught a glimpse of me as she was scanning the beach and she raced over in anger. "I know where you have been." With that death stare rubbed all over her face again like moisturiser.

"Where have I been, Mum?!" Saying it with my arms crossed and body tilted a little bit.

"You went over to the homeless people, didn't you!?" she arched over me, like a tall, strong birch tree towering over an alley.

"Um... yes," I replied in a whimpering voice. But then I had second thoughts of how confident I should be to have helped people. "Do you have a problem with that?!" I spoke with a more powerful voice, on my tiptoes trying to arch over her (it didn't work though).

"You know I do, why do it?!" She placed her hands on my shoulders, pushing me back down.

I was shocked, did she just push me? "Why did you do that? I was helping people. Isn't that how you have raised me? To help people. To be kind," I strongly suggested, trying to put my point across.

"Yes, I did raise you to be kind, but also to listen to me. Were the countless years of me raising you all for nothing? I work hard for our money, we almost didn't come to Australia this year if I hadn't of worked those extra hours all of last month, but you're just throwing it away to these worthless people that just sit there taking other people's money, they're just going to spend that money on drugs you know!? So, thank you for wasting my money." I actually felt quite guilty for a moment. She walked away, whipping her long, bristly hair in my face as she pivoted.

But I remembered that you can't judge books by their covers. "Mum! What do you HATE about these people so much!?"

As I was walking, even chasing after her with my face going like a red hot chilli, I locked my hand on her shoulder trying to slow her pace and she sharply turned around. My life literally flashed before my eyes in a millisecond, it was surreal.

With her lion-like eyes spearing me through the head, Jane SLAPPED me in my face so hard that I fell to my left onto the ground in terror! At first, I didn't feel the pain because of all the adrenaline but the aftermath was horrific, it burned. Jane stared at me. Her face like a finely ripe tomato. Behind her back she held her hand in a fist ready to attack again, well that's what it looked like. My eyes welled up with tears.

"YOU HAVE RUINED MY LIFE AND SO I'M GOING TO RUIN YOURS!" Then she walked like a tornado back towards the house.

I burst out crying, I spoke whilst stumbling to my feet. "What have I done that has made you into a monster!? How have I ruined your life?"

As Jane stopped in her tracks and slowly turned around, the tension that made my stomach twist got worse. I started walking backwards to get further and further away. As an advantage to her, she saw me getting scared which gave her more power and confidence. She stared at me while having a smirk drawn on her face, like something out of a cartoon, which gave a hint that her plan was going perfectly. She walked towards me, slowly through the sand, dragging her feet like a zombie, she looked drugged.

"You have stolen my thunder. You have stolen all of my love, that I used to have." Firmly poking herself in the chest. "You have made me feel terrible as a human, you have made me feel dumb, with your smartness. You have made me stressed with your naughtiness, but yet you get away with it. EVERY TIME."

"But..." I interrupted, with anxiety flowing through my veins.

"Do not interrupt me, EVER! Go be homeless, I don't want you as a daughter anymore, I'm going to adopt another child, but this time I'm choosing what child I want. You are a worthless speck of dust!" She spat. My chocolate brown eyes filled with tears. I felt rage building up inside of me.

"WHAT?!" I roared back. "You be homeless, you dare speak to me like that again I will phone the police, I'm your daughter!" I felt power amongst my bones filling with confidence.

"WHAT? Did you just speak to your mother like that?" Before I had time to answer, Jane was upon me forehead to forehead. I pushed her back with my power that was still building up inside. She swirled her head around in a circle, clicking her neck, looking back at me again. She ran forward and kicked me in the stomach, while punching me in the nose. It was something out of an action movie. I went down like a sack of spuds. Suddenly, the sky went dark, angry birds flew from the trees and waves got more fierce and violent. I couldn't breathe, my nose started dripping out blood like a tap left on.

I called for help and one last time for Jane. The noises in my ears were church bells ringing, crows screeching, children's laughter fading from down the beach. It got me unbalanced and so I fell to the ground, frightened of my surroundings. Shivering and trembling so much on my words I couldn't shout for help anymore. I was covered in blood, my face stung, and my chest ached.

"Jane, I can't breathe, help! Please HELP!" The homeless woman hearing my screams carried me into safety and the man fought against Jane. I guess what goes around comes around.

Rachel, John, Joey and May all ran out to the sound of Jane yelling. Rachel ran over while the others followed but more slowly in hesitation, she yelled, "Hey, what's going on?!"

"They are stopping me from getting to Nova," Jane lied. "Get this slug off me."

"Don't listen to her!" I came out from behind the rocks, with blood all over my face and sand all over the side of my arms and legs, red cheeks and weak legs.

"Oh my gosh, what happened?!" cried Aunt May, in the middle of running over.

"Something is wrong with Jane. She isn't making any sense, she attacked me and it's scaring me." I started crying and the tears started to run down my face one after the other. May hugged me so tight and carried me back carefully.

"Is this true, Jane?" John angrily asked.

"Not a single word! I came over because this stupid man was attacking her!" Jane screamed.

"That's not what Nova said, you liar," answered Uncle Joey.

"Well, she's lying," Jane shouted. John took over holding Jane and thanked the homeless people.

Joey argued, "I don't think Nova would lie about something like this, we all know her way too well. So, tell the truth, Jane." He stood with his arms crossed.

Jane had a cheesy grin appear across her face as she licked her lips like there was a substance there. "I'm telling the truth." She smiled.

Joey went close to her face and kneeled down in the sand. "What drug have you taken, you psychopath?"

"Nothing." She laughed. Rachel called the police and John and Joey stood out front with her waiting to keep her away from me.

Jane managed to break free from John's grip and as she sprinted in the house she found me in the back room guarded by May and Rachel. She shoved May into the wall and punched Rachel in the nose and grabbed my arm violently and yelled in my face, "You're coming with me!"

She locked the door just before the men reached the room. She opened the window, tied a shoelace around my hands and threw me out of the window onto a pile of bricks. I screamed in pain as the brick dug into my side. I was quivering and fought to get loose. I landed badly on my wrist and had full body grazes from the sharpness of the bricks.

Jane jumped out and slapped her hand over my mouth. "Shut up," she whispered in my ear.

She tugged me onto my feet and threw me over her shoulder and sneaked onto the beach and made her way down to the road. I was struggling to scream, with the horror of being killed; tears were dripping onto her shoulder. I was really panicking. No-one was on the beach and no-one at the time was driving on the road.

As all hope was lost for me, I heard a man yell, "Stop walking, and slowly turn around!"

It was the policeman, sprinting down the beach with a Taser ready to zap. As the man caught up, he tried to zap Jane, but she used me as a shield and swung me into him like a cannon ball, and it ended up zapping me. My heart stopped. The terror brought the large vein out in my throat to show the strain.

From there I just slept in the depth of darkness, feeling the motion of an upside-down rollercoaster. Soon I was up again; as soon as my eyes contacted light, I was in the middle of a game of tug-of-war between a policeman and Jane. It's not what you would typically experience every day, my arms ached, and legs gave up. I didn't even try to break free, I just waited to be dropped.

My body was hitting the tipping point of exhaustion and I was feeling the verge of a black-out, before I heard voices scrape the top of the road and that in that moment they sounded like angels. John and Joey came running at Jane, as fierce as lions, they weren't hesitating this time. They now knew what Jane was capable of they did everything to protect me.

I landed on the floor with a salty stream of tears running past my nose onto my collar bone. My spine ached. But the worst part was to see your best friend, mother and protector get beaten up; it killed me inside. My brain was drained. To hear my mother yell for mercy made my ears bleed. But I couldn't move.

"STOP!!" she yelled. "It hurts," she cried.

I was taken away by the arms of a hero that saved my life but scarred my vision. John panted as he reached back home with me. He laid me down on the sofa and collapsed to his knees, slowly rubbing my forehead. "You're safe, Nova." Just before he passed out on the floor beside me, I smiled.

CHAPTER 7

As I awoke from my nightmare, the exhaustion still lingered within the muscle that I had. John was still passed out next to me, but we had both been seen to as we were provided with blankets and cushions and had icepacks on our bodies. My temperature had lowered so much that I shivered, so with my frail fingers I slid the ice off onto the floor next to John. I felt claustrophobic and I was so puny I could barely move the blanket up higher to my ears. I let out a moan as I scraped my cold skin with my sharp nail, and it hurt so much, like a knife scoring the skin. A crowd of nurses herded into the lounge with equipment. I sighed.

Aunt May followed with her slight fingers covering her thin lips.

A couple of minutes had passed where they fed me some food to give power to my muscles. I felt energised and ready to stand up. As the nurses collected their accessories and left the room, May held my hands in a ball and wouldn't let me sit up because she was too worried that I was too scrawny. I pleaded that she would leave the room to give me my space and time to recover, it was hard, but she left to the kitchen after a few moments.

I pulled myself up and strained my neck muscle, letting out a whine. I shut my mouth quickly and crinkled my eyes, remembering to be quiet. I reached for the coat on the chair next to me and swung it over my shoulders. I gave a huge push off the sofa, almost falling forward. Stumbling to my feet, I grabbed hold of the wall and headed to the hallway to the front door. It was raining, pouring, even hailing but I twisted the door handle and pushed. I squinted and took a step still clinging onto the wall. I went faster and faster, taking each step like it was my last. As I heard steps heading to my direction, I swung the door shut. I dragged my feet faster through the gravel, I was desperate to get somewhere peaceful. It was killing me that I couldn't run. I hid behind the neighbour's wall as May frantically ran out yelling my name. Why did I do this? Because I wanted another sign that there was something beyond the skyline, watching over me, to give me hope that something good was going to come out of all of this.

I made my way to the entrance of a great mountain that called my name to get away from the world.

My thighs had become worn out as I reached a third of the way up the hill. I wheezed trying to get extra breaths to carry on. I just couldn't with my weak legs. I soon found a sheltered spot from the horrendous rain that had drowned Sydney. I watched the village down below me, whilst crying. What had I witnessed? Why me? I felt emotionally wrecked and scared that I could never go back from this petrifying holiday.

As I caught my breath, I walked on up this mountain that provided peace. Not having a care in the world of what I was doing because nothing could make this day any worse. I thought to myself, *You don't always need a plan put on paper, you just need to breathe and let go and see where life will take you.* This was all I cared about.

I got too excited to have time to myself. I got lost and grew weaker, I needed food, I was dehydrated, and cold because the coat flew off into the wind as it was only resting on my shoulders. I ended up becoming nauseous because I had pushed myself too hard with my recovery process still in motion.

Not long after, I fell to my knees, slipping down the muddy and rocky hill, tumbling like a brick down an obstacle course. I screamed, panicking to clutch anything to help me from falling; I whimpered, breathing heavily still screaming, crying, heavily freaking out. I was so scared. Soon the falling stopped, as my head hit a tree stump and my fragile back was shredded on a piercing rock collection. The pain was unbearable but was soon gone too quick for me to find myself back in Heaven.

God didn't have to say anything, she just waited for me to spill out with tears. "I'm sorry," I sobbed on the floor. "I helped homeless people, why must good people get hurt?!" I hesitated. "What is wrong with Jane? My mother attacked me." I stood to my feet.

She smiled (which filled me with calmness). "You are so brave..."

"NO... I'm not. Just please put something straight with me," I shouted because I was tired of being pitied for.

"Of course." She felt my pain and didn't want to make matters worse.

"What happened to my mother?"

"My darling, Jane stole the drugs from the hospital and overdosed, which took over and messed with her brain, controlling her insanity."

"What did she take them for?"

"Depression."

"What was she depressed from?"

"Your dad not being around, she misses him. She also had to tell you something but couldn't ruin your relationship, so she kept hiding it."

"Could you tell me?"

"I'll let you find it out for yourself."

"Is it really bad?"

"I can't say anything."

She lifted my head with her hand and looked up into the magnificent sky that was clear blue while taking a deep, deep breath and sharply gazed back at me and before I knew it, God was in my head. I was back in the deep dark alley that was in my dream way before this holiday, remembering where I left off when this treacherous monster was about to gobble me in one bite.

She warmed my hands as I shook with fear. Then she left my head and stared me in the eye and looked guilty.

"I am so sorry. I have put too much horror in your life in such short time, I have been cruel and unfair. It will get much better, I promise."

She held me tight and used her goodness to stop me from shaking. God told me, "You will have one more chance on Earth and if it does not go well, then you may come back to me, and stay with me. I will always be with you, and remember, Jane will love you but she's recovering so she won't think about you for a while, but don't let one person's mistake ruin your life, stay happy, and be grateful for your family because they love you. You can still make a change and be a greater person, I'm on your side."

She blew a kiss to my face and soon I was back ready to take on the world once more.

CHAPTER 8

I peered into the bright light that shone in from between each tree, surprised to see daylight from when I was last there. I was relieved to be full of energy and warmth again although I was still covered in dry mud, my back was miraculously fixed, and my head wasn't pounding. I was ready to see my family and tell them what I wanted to do with my life. I held onto each tree root that was hanging out of the ground for support on the way down; they were like banisters that you would get on a staircase.

As I approached the road just opposite their house, I was having second thoughts of going back from the trouble I had caused, but I knew I had to. I gazed into the blue sky and felt an urge to go on, and so I smiled, breathed, and whispered to the sun, "Wish me luck."

I reached their orange front door surrounded by police cars; I had a think of what to say. *I've got it!* I knocked on the door. I was standing there like a lemon full of adrenaline. I waited there for a few minutes and there was nothing. I pressed my face upon their matted window next to the door. There was no movement whatsoever.

I had a think and I had an idea.

I walked around the back, between the wooden fence and the holly bush and came upon a gate with a code. "OH NO!" I yelled, ducking under the window out of sight. "What am I going to do?" I whispered; I didn't know their code. I didn't even know they even had a gate, I thought it was all open.

In the corner of my eye I saw a ditch. I remember John telling me a funny story of a stray fat cat scrambling through their fence to catch a bird. You know I didn't particularly like the cat because it had destroyed a lot of things in my family's garden, but I'm a big believer that everything happens for a reason, and this stupid cat will help me reach my family for a very important reason. So, thank you fat cat.

I got onto my hands and knees like the creature, and tried to crawl through; this is where I wish I didn't eat those extra couple of pancakes and sweets a couple of days ago, because otherwise I could fit. I had to think of another idea because I was quite hungry, and my limbs started to numb.

I pushed to my feet, whilst wiping leaves and dry mud off me. I turned my head to the left and in my horror, I was to see a pigeon with one wing just in front of me. How did I not see this before? I screamed to my disgust and fell onto my ankle, letting out a cry of pain. Julia heard my scream and opened up the gate and gasped with delight. She sprung herself upon me and quickly stood up, remembering I was in recovery and my bones were marshmallows. She pulled me to my feet and placed my arm around her shoulder and walked me into the garden.

As I entered, I found Rachel crying, and Aunt May rubbing her back explaining that everything will be OK. May turned her head over into my direction and gasped in happiness. "NOVA!" All of a sudden, the sky went bluer, the clouds disappeared, the waves got larger, the sand got warmer and best of all May smiled which warmed my heart. I knew God was with me at this very moment.

Rachel turned around slowly, and her dark chocolate eyes filled with tears of joy. Rachel leaped from her chair, knocking it down, and sprinted over and hugged me as tight as possible. Then of course

May joined in. "Where are the men?" I asked (Michael didn't understand any of this drama so was happily playing on the beach).

"Well, John has gone to hospital and, well Joey, has…"

"John has gone to hospital?" What have I done?

"Yes, honey. Rachel will tell you what happened to Joey later, but we are both so happy that you are back and safe." May always made me feel less guilty.

I wiped the tears off their faces and suggested that we all go inside. After having a lovely cold cup of lemonade, because it was boiling hot outside, I had a long shower, getting all the sand, mud and blood off. I was a mess.

I wore a denim all-in-one jumpsuit and a white crop top underneath, with denim summer shoes and white socks. My hair was put in two French plats by Julia and she even added summer flowers to look pretty and to look like I had tried to look aesthetically pleasing to see John at the hospital.

Aunt May drove in their orange Range Rover through the winding lanes to the hospital that was only three miles away. Julia and Michael stayed home with their tutors for school. It was silent in the car. Rachel sat in the back with me and we held hands all the way.

As we approached, Rachel was shaking, even finding it hard to talk. "I don't want to go in. I'll start crying again. It's too hard." Rachel gazed out of the window, blinking hard to get rid of the tears.

"Nova and I will go in and you come in when you feel like it. OK?" May said, placing her hand on her knee as she leaned back from the driver's seat.

Rachel just nodded; no words were spoken after that. I accidently slammed the door as I got out making Rachel jump. I mimed 'Sorry' through the window, she just smiled so I smiled back. May reached for my hand and squeezed it tight, guiding me through the front door.

She stopped walking and said, "Nova. John is in, well, a BAD state right now. I don't want how he looks to scare you when you walk in. OK?"

"OK." I nodded with my hand slipping out of Aunt May's as the nerves started to kick in and my palms became sweaty.

"I just want you to be warned, just in case." I nodded, looking around to see my surroundings.

We reached the reception and asked for the keys to his room; for some reason John does not like a lot of visitors, so he asked them to lock his room when the doctors aren't there. The hospital was, well, busy with nurses and doctors rushing around, there was the hospital smell with sick mixed with hand sanitiser. Although it was quite posh for a hospital and quite clean.

As the receptionist went into the room behind her to get the keys, May looked down and bit her lip. "It may look a bit manic in here, but it is lovely and quiet in John's room, so you can have a peaceful chat, OK?"

Then she looked back up reaching over the counter for the keys from the receptionist as she placed them on the desk.

I slotted the keys into the lock and slowly turned my hand and waited to hear a click. The door creaked open and, in this moment, I couldn't bear to see what I saw again.

To my horrifying shock, John looked as if he had been beaten. Dry blood and long deep cuts all over his face, down his arms, even down his stomach. I couldn't believe that I was the reason for this. I would have to live with this for the rest of my life.

I sharply turned around; May tried to stop me but I slipped out of her reach and ran out into the boys' toilets by accident, and slammed the door shut. I walked around the corner and pressed my back against the wall and slid down slowly. I rested my head on my knees.

I kept on breathing heavily and saying quietly, "This can't be happening right now, THIS CAN'T! THIS IS ALL MY STUPID FAULT!"

An old man came out from the cubicle with his old wooden walking stick and was really puzzled. He washed his hands, keeping his eyes on me. He checked the toilet symbol again, so he was sure that this was the boys' toilets, and he wasn't going crazy. He walked back in and said, "Young lady?"

I lifted my head and my eyes widened, questioning in my mind, 'Why was a man in the girl's bathroom?'

"Yes?" I looked puzzled.

"These are the men's toilets."

"What? I think you are mistaken, sir, these are the ladies' toilets."

He opened the door and showed me the symbol.

"Oh. Thanks for telling me." Embarrassment just filtered throughout my whole body.

"It's OK. You should be more aware in the future, young lady." Putting his point across.

He stood there holding the door open, waiting for me to go. I smiled and walked into the room next to the boys' toilets which were the girls' toilets, while hiding my face so no one would know it was me. I grabbed some tissue and taking a deep breath I strolled back into John's room.

May turned around looking quite red and stormed over to me, grabbing my arm and taking me outside for a chat. "Where have you been?"

"I was scared when I saw John like this, so I ran into the toilets to get some tissue and thought about what I should say when he wakes up," I whispered.

We both heard a yawning sound behind us. We turned around

sharply, while our eyes widened, and tip-toed back in the room closing the door behind us.

"May? Is that you?" questioned John.

"Hi, I have a surprise for you." May stepped aside and I was in his sight.

"Nova! How are you? It's great to have you back!"

"Hi John. I am feeling great," I lied, "...it's great for me to see you again." I tried to smile but nothing appeared.

"Nova what's wrong?" he questioned, looking concerned.

I sprinted over beside his bed and hugged him. "I'm so sorry. I did this to you."

"Hey. It wasn't your fault."

"Yes, it was. I was the one to run away. I was the one who brought you into this position. If it wasn't me who ran away, we would all be on the beach right now having lemonades. I'm so sorry! I am such an IDIOT. John I will make this up to you, I will!" I stared into his eyes that were filled with happiness.

"You may have cursed us with worriedness, but this was nowhere near your fault. You know what?" Grabbing my hands and holding them tight.

"What?" I tilted my head because he looked so happy.

"This was all Jane's fault. Because Jane hurt you, which made you upset and run away which was understandable, so you could have some time to think to yourself without anybody else distracting you or making matters worse, I mean I would've done the exact same thing. So, if Jane didn't upset you, this whole scenario would never have happened."

"You're right. This is Jane's fault." I wiped my tears off my face and sat in the chair next to his bed. A few hours passed and we chatted about how he got all his cuts.

"Well, I fell in bramble bush because I tripped over a stick, yes, I'm that clumsy." We both laughed. "Then as I spotted you halfway up the mountain I called for your name but you were too far away, so I ran and slipped, again, but this time on slippery and watery mud and flew down a rocky bank landing in a vicious river with all sorts of rubbish flying into my face. Some parts were from the car garage down the road, so I have some metal scrapes too." He was a real hero to me.

Then I told him what happened to me, about landing on a tree stump and rocks. I was thinking of telling him about my further experience or just my experience in general with God, but I thought to myself that it would be mine and God's little secret.

We talked like there was no tomorrow and after two hours Rachel showed up and we all had a lovely chat, we laughed and told strange stories and talked about what would happen next and where I would go, but there was only one solution. Soon after, we were locking the door and heading out to go back home, leaving John in the hospital to rest.

"That was lovely, Nova," May spoke, placing her arm around my shoulder, while heading outside back to the car. "That really was. You may have been scared at first, but you held it in and reassured John that you were OK, that's all that he would ask for."

"Thanks, May. Thanks to you too, Rachel, for bringing me here, I am really sorry to both of you. I should have had more common sense not to run away, I love you guys." We had a group hug which seems cringy to say now but it felt so special at the time.

We stopped at the car and jumped in. I placed my seat belt on and sunk into the car seat watching all the birds race with us, gliding through the wind, swooping in and out of palm trees, now this was something out of a movie.

"Nova, would you like to go back to your original home tomorrow?" Rachel announced. "You must be tired of it here. Maybe I can stay with you for a few weeks until something is sorted out?"

"It's not that I'm tired of it here, I just miss home." Thinking about my room full of secrets and my special bench that I go to every Saturday, to think about my sister in the navy and my dad travelling the world. "I think I want to go back home, yeah; I want to go home." Placing my head on the window. Happily sighing.

"OK then, I'll book tickets for the plane."

We arrived back home, had drinks and went to bed ready for my journey back home. I was really going to miss this place; I now have a crazy story to tell. I wonder what's next for me; hopefully something good.

I laid down in bed and gazed at the ceiling full of thoughts. I was excited to go back home, I was nervous of the thought that anything can happen, but overall I felt safe that now I knew God is with me in whatever I do. I blew kiss to the window knowing that God would catch it and take it with her for the night. As I closed my eyes, I smiled ready for the next chapter.

CHAPTER 9

As the sun reached over the horizon and the smooth waves crashed ashore, Rachel walked in at 6:30am and sat on the end of my bed with a warm cup of green tea. She waited patiently for me to sit up, with a smile on her face. She knew the tough couple of days I'd just had so she wanted to make me feel a hundred times better. I stretched my arms wide into the air and crawled on the bed with my weak legs and gave her a hug from behind, trying not to spill the tea that she held. I swung my legs over the side of the bed and let them dangle as we had a positive morning conversation to get ready for the journey.

Soon May came crashing through the door with excitement and enthusiasm because it was such a beautiful day outside. She is a big believer that the weather helps change your mood, so she danced around the room with some burning sage to "get rid of the evil spirits" that she felt were "lingering" from the past couple of days. She picked up my tea and placed it on the table close by and dragged me into the bathroom (still dancing).

"I know this might be hard, but forget about all of the horrendous nightmares you've just had and freshen up, OK? I have loads of products for you to use and as soon as you come out breakfast will be ready." She skipped out. I walked to the door and locked it tight.

I walked out of the shower with my hair dripping everywhere and flipped it over my head. I lathered body lotion and skin oil all over me and brushed my teeth.

Suddenly, as I had finished combing my hair, out of the corner of my eye I saw a photo. I picked up the picture from behind the sink; I don't really know who would hide a photo in a room where it's going to get wet but, oh well.

As my vision focused it was a picture of Jane and a man kissing. I dropped it into a pool of water, it sunk to the bottom and I just stared at it. Jane looked the same as she did now in the photo, so I picked it up from the deep water and checked the back. It was taken a couple of weeks ago!

The background looked like the entrance to her work and it was late at night; this explains why she stayed late all of those days, not to earn money for us to go on holidays, but to cheat on my father! That psycho is going to pay! I had SO many questions. Firstly, who is this man?

I stormed out of the bathroom, leaving the window open so the door slammed right behind me. I was so angry, "What is this?!"

I forgot to hold my towel and I dropped it in front of Rachel in the kitchen. "OH MY GOD!" Then I dropped the picture and I ran out scrunching up my towel. As I locked the door in the guest bedroom, Rachel came yelling to ask where I'd found this.

"Nova! Come out!" she demanded. I came storming out with an over-sized t-shirt and pyjama shorts on. I walked angrily into the lounge.

"So, May, what was that about forgetting all of my unluckiness from the last few days, huh?" I stood with my arms crossed.

"Excuse me?" She placed down her newspaper. Rachel came in red faced. I snatched it off her and made the photo very visible. "WHERE DID YOU FIND THIS, NOVA!?" She shot up from her chair.

"That's not the point, May! It's the fact that you were trying to make me forget about all of the terrible events that have just happened and then you go and put another one in my life, why?" My face welled up.

"Nova, I..." Then she realised that I was truly damaged and didn't need any more shouting, so she calmed down. "I didn't know that this photo was in this house, I knew it existed and I yelled at your mother for doing this, I don't know how or why it's here."

"Well, as soon as I thought that it was just this holiday that my mother has done wrong, I'm guessing I was very inaccurate. My poor dad, he was only supporting our family, and then my mum just has to go and cheat on him," I cried. "Wait... God told me that Jane was taking these drugs for depression, from not seeing Jaimie in over a year, so as she cheated on him she must have noticed that this was terribly wrong and didn't know how to control her feelings so she took her anger out on me. Is this what God was telling me? I guess I've just figured out why she overdosed on the hospital tablets."

"What?!" Rachel clenched my arm. "Who told you this?" I stayed quiet. Staring into her eyes, I didn't want to get into another argument about if God was real or not.

She shrugged my arm, so I was swung to my left. Still holding on to my arm she demanded an answer. I know she wasn't trying to hurt me. "Nova! Tell me!" My head dropped.

"Just leave me alone for once!" I tried to walk away, but she pulled me back. I felt trapped, like I couldn't escape her claws.

"Alright, Rachel that's enough!" May yelled. "She's gone through enough; Nova doesn't need any more. Can't you understand her pain?" She broke the link between Rachel's hand and my arm.

"I'm sorry." I stormed out, shaking. "NOVA! I'm sorry." May stopped Rachel from chasing after me. "What are you doing? She's going to run away again."

"She won't. She's learned her lesson. She knew what happened last time. She knew what happened to everyone, that it wasn't just her getting hurt. She just needs to be alone, give her space," May calmingly said.

Rachel ripped her arm back from May and stormed out to the kitchen. May knocked gently on my door. "Hey, it's me. Can I come in?"

I walked to the door, unlocked it and slowly it creaked open. "I just want the pain to go away." I broke down in tears, sliding to the floor. May caught me and helped walk me to the edge of my bed.

"I promise it will. Rachel was only trying to help."

"How? By yelling at me? I'm on thin ice, I can't do this anymore. I'm tired. I just want to go home, just take me home. Please."

Rachel leaned at the door frame watching with tears streaming down her face. I saw her and opened my arm for her to come over. She ran and squeezed me so tight. "I'm so sorry, my darling. I was stupid, insensitive and cruel. I promise to protect you and treat you right. Can you forgive me?"

I looked over and smiled with weary lips. "Of course, I can."

As we sat for a couple of minutes, Rachel remembered we had a plane to catch, so we ran all over the house gathering our belongings.

I dried my hair, and wore a short white silk dress, with white flats and curly hair.

It was 8:27am and we packed the car, gathered some snacks and said our goodbyes. I really didn't want to leave, with the sounds of the beach, a supportive family and Michael giving me goodbye presents like a 'See you soon' card and Julia giving me a massive hug and May crying not wanting to let me go. It seemed like a fairy tale, to me it was. It really was a moment to remember.

We got in the car and waved goodbye from the front passenger window. (We were in their orange range rover.)

Five minutes into the car ride Rachel told me about Joey.

"Nova, I think it's time I tell you what happened to Uncle Joey. Is that OK?"

"Yeah, I think so, I think I'm ready. I'm not sure if I'm ready for any more bad news, but right now I just want to know."

"Honey, if you're not sure I can tell you another time, I mean we have two weeks together."

"I know, but these two weeks will go way too fast, so I'm ready!" I replied. Rachel coughed to clear her throat and gripped hard onto the steering wheel.

"OK. Just prepare yourself for bad news." I nodded, taking a deep breath. "Joey, well he obviously went after you, with the hope of finding you."

"Oh no. Oh no. Oh no. What have I done! I killed him, didn't I? I knew it!" I started bashing my head against the car window.

"Nova! What? Stop doing that! You're going to hurt yourself."

"What happened to him?"

"So, he spotted you a third up the hill and ran because he saw you fall. He slipped on the murky floor and slammed his head on a rock. He then was unconscious and started to tumble down the hill and got airlifted to Singleton Hospital in Swansea. I know it's far away, but they had so many things they could do for him there. That's why I was so worried about you because I thought you did the same and we couldn't find you." Rachel gripped even harder onto the steering wheel, holding back her tears and biting her quivering lip.

"Oh my gosh. But I was the cause of it."

"We just wanted to keep you safe."

"Well, next time don't, I can't lose one of you due to my stupidity."

"We love you way too much to—"

"Stop loving me then… Please. If I put your life on the line for loving me, then stop loving me."

"That'll never happen, do you understand how hard it is to stop loving someone? It's an honour to protect you and I will always protect you, even if at the time I hate you, which is also impossible, I will be there, for you," she yelled, kindly.

"OK, I get it. I love you too," I replied. "But I'm still the cause of it," I whispered under my breath.

"Nova! No one cares who caused it, it is always the person's fault who carried it on. Joey didn't have to climb up that mountain after you. He had two choices, but he did and that's his fault, not yours."

"Yeah, well at the end of the day, it is my FAULT!" I screamed.

"Look, I'm trying to be positive. With my sister and brother-in-law in hospital and jail, how am I supposed to keep calm? With you yelling and blaming yourself for everything, how am I supposed to control you? How am I supposed to keep you sane? How am I supposed to know what to say to a damaged girl? How am I supposed to—"

"Alright, I GET IT! I get it." I broke the noise. "You have never been in this situation before and neither have I. I'm a teenager and you're a grown woman with your own kids, how am I supposed to know what to do? I just feel like bashing my head on a rock. No one understands my pain, my broken soul. I don't want to be controlled, I want to know what to do, but I can't think of anything. Alright, just calm down and let's just focus on getting there before we get in a car crash!" I was angry. Fuming. The car was dead silent after that. Just the sound of passing cars. Seconds later I started to feel extremely warm, sweaty warm.

"Whoa is it just me or is it hot in here?"

"Not really but, turn down your window." It didn't really help.

"Could we visit Joey when we get there?"

"Of course." A smile appeared on Rachel's face when she knew we were having a genuine conversation again.

CHAPTER 10

Suddenly, I started to shake. My heart was pumping faster and faster with the warmth of the blood boiling, my knees were clashing uncontrollably, hairs were standing on edge and my eyes started to glitch. Jane's voice came back from a memory to haunt, it terrorised me. Soon I was going pale as I looked in the side window. "Rachel, I don't feel so great!" I grabbed her arm that was resting and clenched it.

"Nova! You're scaring me, what's wrong?" Rachel started to slow the car down. "Nova, it's OK to breathe, in and out, come on, with me, in and out. Are you cold? Do you need a drink? What do you feel like? Do you feel faint? Nova, talk to me."

"I'm scared." I turned cold and shivered.

"It's going to be fine, alright, keep breathing. We are so close to the airport, just keep breathing."

"Yeah but I'm scared. I'm cold, I can't breathe normally. Rachel, help."

"It's alright, Nova. Close your eyes and imagine you on an island, far away, where you can hear waves, wind blowing through the trees and birds chirping. Focus on those sounds," she said gently.

Suddenly, my heart rate went back to normal, I was warm again and my terror feelings were gone. I opened my eyes and my hand relaxed from squeezing Rachel's arm. I glanced forward. "What just happened?"

"Are you OK, Nova?"

"I'm better."

"Great. But what just happened?"

"I felt trapped, like the world was closing in on me and Jane's voice was on repeat disturbing me. I felt like something was coming after me, the whole climate changed, it went from boiling in a sauna to freezing in an ice bath. I was nauseous, everything went blurry. I'm scared if it comes back again."

"Well you are OK now. Alright, remember to breathe. The airport is a minute away, when we get there we can go to the nurse and check you out."

"No nurse, I just want to get home."

"The nurse won't delay our flight, it's just a check-up."

"No, I will just follow your instructions. To breathe."

As we entered the gates, Rachel parked in long-stay parking. I jumped out of the car and viewed the planes speeding off the ground into the air, splitting the air particles in half as they sawed through the sky. When I thought of coming back home on a plane, I didn't think it would be with Rachel. Although, I did like the feeling of being with somebody else because you get a different experience of the airport, and besides there was no panicked situations; Rachel was totally calm and made the whole airport seem like a playground with no rushing.

I pulled my suitcase out from the boot along with my other mini suitcase. I placed the neck pillow around the handle and helped Rachel with her travelling bags. I rolled the wheels on the concrete as we headed to terminal three, and it made the sound I love; this to me is the sound of adventure, although it was very noisy and disturbing and even drew attention from fellow travellers, it just got me excited. We entered and headed straight for the check-in area.

After that, we travelled to the hand-in luggage desks. They were very sweet ladies, considering the amount of people present. Then, the adults' "favourite" (sarcastic voice) part of the whole process, security.

This did slow us down by thirty minutes. So, to pass the time Rachel and I shared headphones and jammed to music. The guy who served us during security was very intimidating and rude to us, I mean we were just following everyone else. Rachel gave him the cold shoulder before we left just to give him an idea of how he was treating everyone else.

We didn't go straight to the food shops, we actually searched for our boarding gate just to know where it was, so we didn't have to rush when it was near the time to go. Amazingly, as we approached our gate, there was a lush restaurant and toilets opposite. We literally jumped with joy. What a coincidence! This took a lot of pressure and rushing off our shoulders. Well, Rachel's.

Rachel headed to the toilets and I sat down with the on-board luggage at a sofa and coffee table. It was very modern, they had grey walls, with black sofas and seats, glass tables and marble counters. I got really comfortable contemplating the time we had left before our plane was boarding people. Just to put in perspective, we had two hours.

As I was minding my own business, scrolling through pictures of Jane, I turned my mobile data on to watch a happy memory video of last summer we were here in Australia, and then came through hundreds of messages from May sending her love. I think she lost control of the GIFs because half of them were of sending love. I laughed and sent loads back. I'm glad she wants to keep me happy. I forgot where I was for a minute and I put my feet on the table and relaxed.

You would never guess what happened next; you know when you look somewhere random and just start to daydream, so aren't actually focussed on what you're looking at? Well, as my sight focussed as I dropped my phone onto my stomach, I had been staring at the cutest boy I had ever seen, for a minute straight. It appeared that he was also staring back, don't know for how long, but for long enough that I caught him. I immediately took my feet off the table and curled up on the sofa in embarrassment. I was only so weakened because I was an outcast in school and all boys just stayed away. I hated school, not for that but just for the awful people that treated me like dirt. Anyway, I just stared at my phone and kept scrolling.

Thankfully, Rachel walked in all freshened. "Before I sit down, what do you want to eat and drink?" She searched for her purse in her bag.

"Can I have a mango smoothie, and camembert with olive bread dip? Please," I smiled.

"Hey, feet off the sofa silly girl." She laughed. As she went to the till, I quickly glanced over to the boy and he was writing something. I thought it was some sort of schoolwork, so I went back to texting Julia about this guy, asking her what to do.

"Just go over and talk to him." This really didn't help. Anyway, I was never going to see him again, so why not? I took a deep breath and was about to stand up before Rachel called over across the cafe.

"Nova. They don't have a mango smoothie, which other one do you want?!" I got so humiliated; I could definitely see the boy looking at me now.

"Any other one, Rachel," I quietly responded.

"What?!"

I just got up and walked over. "I'll have the green smoothie, please," I asked the cashier. Then I walked back, I walked past the boy's table and he stood up.

"Um, hey," he nervously said.

I turned around like I was waiting for this to happen. "Hey," I said friendlily.

"Could you read this for me, when you sit down?" He handed me a piece of paper with a poem.

"Of course." I sat down and read it.

This isn't a poem,
I just want to ask you; how do you ask a girl out?
I thought you would know because I'm sure a boy has asked you out before.

Part of me was disappointed, I didn't get a poem. Although my heart did warm when he mentioned a boy asking me out, does this mean that he thinks I'm pretty? Now this is where I mess up. I have no clue what to do now. I wish I had an answer for his question, but I have nothing. I am no love expert and I have never felt so clueless in my life.

I saw him staring over here, looking nervous. Now I knew we were both in the same boat of anxiety, I just had to be the bigger person and start a conversation. I walked over and handed the piece of paper back.

"I wish I could give you an answer, but I don't know." I hesitated; he looked down at the table. "I mean, what I would like if a boy asked me out is, compliments. Everyone loves compliments, you just have to be smooth talking and don't overthink it because that's when you mess up." His dimples appeared in his cheeks as he smiled.

"Thanks, but what would I do if I didn't know what to say? Because she made me nervous." I could see him look at my lips.

"Look, can I sit here?" He nodded and moved his computer out of the way. "All you have to do is give her compliments, be a gentleman and bring in some humour. A girl loves to laugh."

"Alright, can I practice? On you?"

"Of course, just keep calm, the worst that can happen is that she says 'no'. This is a sign that she's not good enough for you, and you deserve something better. No matter what happens, a girl will realise that you're nervous and will feel honoured that you have tried. Girls are kind like that."

"OK, here goes nothing. What's your name?"

"Nova."

He put his hands on his knees. "Nova, I've been thinking about something for a while and didn't really know how to tell you."

"OK."

"You are the prettiest girl I've ever seen, and you have the kindest heart and a bright mind, that keeps me thinking that I am so lucky to have you as a friend." I smiled; I wished that this would be me someday.

"Thanks." I carried it on.

"I can't stop thinking about you. I tell everyone about you and how great you are."

"What are you trying to say?"

"I love you."

"OK, wait." I was shaking. "You don't say love until you've been going out for a couple of weeks at least. In fact, a couple of months, for some people it takes years, love is like creating a masterpiece, it takes time. Love is too strong. Liking someone and loving someone are two completely different things. So maybe just say, 'I like you' or 'I have feelings for you'."

"But what happens if I really love her?"

"Well, after a couple of months dating and you're sure. Then you say it. You could say it too early and then in a couple of weeks not even like her and leave her, making the girl believe that it was all fake, that could actually damage her. So, you're doing it for her sake."

"OK, thanks. This makes more sense."

I saw Rachel back at the table waiting with our order. "Well, it was nice meeting you. I hope it goes well when you see her." I walked away having a huge grin on my face, excited that I had talked to a boy.

"Oh, wait!" he called back. I turned around. "Can I ask you something?"

"Yeah, of course."

"Will you go out with me?"

I died for a second.

"What? Me? Why? We just met."

"That was a practice, I never actually got around to asking it when we did the role play."

"Oh, ha ha. Yeah, I forgot, I didn't know we were still doing it." I laughed awkwardly.

"No worries. Thanks anyway, coach." He rubbed the back of his head in embarrassment as I turned around and walked away.

I whispered to myself, "Coach? What's that supposed to mean?"

I sat down with Rachel and she looked at me while sipping her tea. "So, who's the boy?" I HATE it when people always assume that something is going on with a boy every time I talk to them, or even bring them up in a conversation. Can girls and boys not talk anymore without being assumed as a couple or a crush?

I looked over and I saw him smile.

"Nothing, Rachel. When can we board?"

"Honey, we still have over an hour before the gates even open. Have some food, OK?"

"OK."

"It looks like you have a crush on him." She saw my blushing cheeks.

"What gave it away?"

She looked at me which emphasised her obviousness. "The rosy cheeks did."

"Wait, did I just admit it? I didn't even think twice!" I even surprised myself.

Rachel laughed. Then we sat back and enjoyed our time before they started announcing the gates.

CHAPTER 11

"Now calling second class, seats 40-55 to board the plane 506, remember to bring all your belongings with you. We shall take off in twenty minutes, thank you." The time had come.

"That's us," I said, standing up.

"This is it, Nova, say goodbye to Australia." We carried our bags over, handed in our boarding passes and walked down the corridor. I loved these corridors, you're either walking onto a plane or walking into a different country. I was greeted with a friendly smile of an air hostess. She guided us to our seats with directions. We ended up being dead on in the middle of the plane. We were on the left-hand side with an aisle seat. Perfect.

I sat on the aisle seat and strapped in. Rachel did the same and reached for my hand because she was also nervous of flying but didn't want to show it in front of me. I smiled, holding her hand, and rested my head on her shoulder.

All of sudden once everybody was strapped in and bags were locked away, the plane engine rumbled beneath us and the wheels started rolling. I leaned forward to gaze out of the window and see the planes nearby. Then after five minutes of turning and reversing, we were on the runway. Rachel gripped me tight, I loved this part. It made me feel exhilarated! I always felt like I was in an action movie. As I've said before.

The plane started collecting speed and the engine was erupting and soon the plane was a racing car and then we were off into the sky. I sat back and laughed; I was living life finally. I was genuinely happy in this moment.

An hour into our flight our food had just arrived that we ordered half an hour ago. As Rachel went to the toilet, I was left alone sitting, reading my book, when I heard a lady cry to my right.

I looked over and she was holding a baby, I wondered if she was just stressed from mothering. She saw me looking and stood up with the child and walked over.

"I'm sorry if I have caused you any disturbance."

"Oh my gosh, no. You haven't, I was just wondering if I could help." I stood up.

"That would be wonderful, could you hold my child while I go and get some medication?" She handed me the baby. She was so beautiful, small and smooth.

"Of course. I can hold her for however long you need."

She smiled and rushed to the bathroom. I smiled at the baby and sat back down. In my bag I had a small neck pillow. I asked a man if he would help me get it out. He did and he put the bag back for me. There were some really nice people on this flight. I sat back down again and placed the baby's head and neck on the pillow, and then I tucked its blanket around its small body to keep it warm because it was very cold on this craft. I felt like a real mother, I loved this.

Then Rachel came back and was in shock. "Who's is this?"

"A woman's, she was stressed, so she's gone to get medication while I hold her."

"What a lovely thing to do."

"Before you sit down, I'll get up and walk around because my legs ache." I lifted myself to my feet and stretched my legs. As Rachel sat down, I walked slowly down the aisle patting the baby's back.

Then after walking around for a couple minutes, I decided to go back.

Then the unimaginable happened. When you thought things couldn't get worse.

The plane dropped and I flew straight to the ceiling, knocking my head on the board. I used my body as a shield for the baby and held tight even though I was scared for my life. I heard screaming, I smelt burning. Then the lights flickered on and off, and as the plane became steady, I fell to the ground onto my back. I screamed in pain. "My back!"

I did my best to scramble to my feet still holding the baby, but now the baby was crying, blasting the high-pitched scream into my ears.

I tried talking to the baby like it was my child, holding my back uncomfortably, "It's OK, stop crying."

As the plane was still, I tried to run back, but gravity's force yanked me down onto my hands and knees, then the plane shook itself. I was thrown to my right whacking my head onto the seat leg. Then thrown to my left hitting my spine on someone's boot cast.

"HELP!" I screamed in mercy. A lady reached for my t-shirt but missed. "PLEASE!" Then an air hostess realised that I was not in a seat, strapped down. Then when she saw the baby, she screamed.

I saw her try to undo her safety belt. "DON'T UNDO YOUR SEATBELT!" I yelled at her to keep her safe, I couldn't let someone die for me. My mission was to keep this baby alive, my second baby step to saving the world. "STAY THERE!" I ordered, even though I wanted the help so bad, I just couldn't be responsible for something like that. I was the only person out of my seat. Everyone was too busy getting their loved ones safe first. I was so vulnerable.

"Nova!" came a scream surprisingly quite clear comparing to the sea of other screaming parents and crying babies.

It was Rachel, worried for my life. I couldn't stand up, I army crawled as far as I could, but my back was aching, my head was pounding, and I was shaking so much I couldn't use my arms to pull myself by the seat legs. Before long I would get dragged back as the plane would bounce vertical, it was a real climb for my life. I was getting really tired, but I couldn't just fall and let this baby die.

I couldn't shout as my voice was too quiet in the volume of fear, I was so horrified that my crackly voice wouldn't get through the crowd. I had no hope, gripping onto the baby, crying. I whispered into her ears, "I'm so sorry. You deserve so much better."

I eventually managed to drag myself onto an empty seat in the front row, but I was facing the back rest and clenching onto it, because if I turned around I would fall forward with no chair to help support me. The baby was laying on my stomach, I had to balance her because I had no extra hands, I was just praying in this very moment.

I was shaking, with blood from my back and head. I knew this was the end. But I had one last thing to do. Tell Rachel I loved her. As much as I had said it, I never thought she knew I meant it. I took a deep breath, let go of the seat, but gripped onto the arm rest, and I slowly lowered myself to the floor, I would use the seat legs as ladders. I didn't climb just yet, from the lady behind, she had a scarf in her bag on the floor. I whipped it from her and made an awful, but better than nothing, harness for the baby to be held on my chest, so had extra hands. It took a while as my hands were terribly shaking. Then with all my power and strength I pulled my way up the vertical plane back to Rachel. I had nothing to lose, other than this child and she was my first priority. Gripping onto the seat legs pulling my way up, I was almost there with her in my sight. But tragedy struck.

From the atmospheric force the plane got ripped in half, right across the centre. I grabbed hold of the seat leg, screaming in horror. It was surreal, it was the scariest thing that I wouldn't wish on anybody. I was on the edge of the of the front side of the plane. Looking over onto the sea. As it snapped, the plane came down like a tornado. It wouldn't stop spinning. I was hanging on with my last muscle, I was screaming to God, "MAKE IT STOP!"

It lasted forever. My legs were thrown into the rip of the plane, where all of the metal structure and wires were, my leg got caught on a sharp spear from the structure and it tore my skin, luckily only the first couple of layers, but it was excruciating as blood was scattered everywhere.

Then the plane slowly stopped spinning and was just free falling in a straight line. As I was steady, I was able to look down, still holding on, to see what we were heading for; all you could see was the sea, utter blue depths.

I then remembered that Rachel was on that other side, being chucked around like a spinning top. Rachel was safe in her seat but not so safe with the situation. She was gone from my reach; I could never hold her hand again or say, 'I love you'.

Both parts of the plane were plummeting to the ground. Like a race to death. We were above the Indian Ocean. The freezing depth of the water would kill us, like a thousand knives stabbing us for every second we were in there. There was no way out. It turned to rain with dark skies and grey dull clouds, the sun was leaving me too. No one on this half of the plane cared about me. They had their loved ones; they had their priorities. I didn't. I couldn't wait any longer. This nightmare was getting more surreal by the second; I started thinking about every single family member, I thought about the fact that I could never have kids, never get married. My life was over. I just mentally prepared myself for death.

A woman saw me hanging there vulnerable, I didn't know that she had tied herself to the chair and was about to unplug herself. As I looked back down about to give up, I felt a vibration from the floor, so looked up and there she was, flat on the floor, reaching for my hand. As soon as our fingertips made contact a huge gust of wind swept me from the plane as my arm muscles had finally given up.

The lady let out a cry of terror as she tried to jump forward and grab me, but she got thrown to the ceiling and was finding it hard to untie herself from the knot she had made. In slow motion, I saw the woman getting smaller and smaller, my hair fluttering beside my ears violently, my arms around the baby, my legs above my head. This was it.

Before I could even blink, the lady jumped out after me, I don't think she even thought twice. She came down like an eagle catching its prey, arms beside her side with legs straight, she looked like a superhero.

As she caught hold of my leg, she pulled herself up to my face, and wrapped herself around me like a piggy in a blanket. Also holding the baby, she swung us around so she would hit the water first, but just before we hit the water's surface, a large piece of metal hit my back making me lose grip of the baby and throwing me out of this lady's grip. The baby landed safe in the water with the woman, but I was far away, with a broken back. Or it felt like it anyway.

"Ahhh. HELP. PLEASE!" I felt trapped, isolated and frightened of what was in the sea. "MY BACK!" The pain was all I could think about, I wasn't at all comfortable, I was ferociously paddling to stop myself from drowning but then I remembered to float on my back like a starfish. It hurt but it would save my life. I laid there for a few seconds before I heard yelling.

"BABY!?" I thought this was Rachel, but it didn't sound like her. I just yelled back.

"OVER HERE."

Soon the woman came speedily swimming with a baby on her back towards me. As she reached me, she said to stay still. She blew up her instant pop-up life jacket that she grabbed before jumping and she threw me onto it. It kept my head above water, and I could stop paddling. She made a DIY life jacket with her puffy coat for the baby to lay on and told me to breathe and to think happy thoughts; amazingly the baby was now asleep so we had some calm sounds of the ocean, well, other than the screams from other surviving passengers.

"I'm so scared." I panicked. "I'm going to die." I was still panicking. She held my hands and reassured me.

"I know it's too late to say this but, if you get a thought of panic or death in your head you'll die. So, keep your faith, like your number one priority, don't let it slip your mind, you're safe now and the baby's safe, you are such a hero." Everything she said was a blur from all the background noise. As I eventually calmed myself down, I looked her in the eye, and she had the exact colours and shapes as mine and her lips were thin and beautiful, like mine. Her nose was like a button, again like mine. She just looked like the older version of me. *Am I being delusional?*

"What? Why are you looking at me like that?" She smiled.

"You look exactly like me; I didn't notice before. I don't know if it is the experience we have just encountered, by making me hallucinate. But you look like me," I stated.

"That's right. You don't know how long I have been looking for you." She hesitated and teared up. "You are my baby, Isabella." She had trembling lips and then she treaded on the water and planted her hand on my cold cheek and looked me in the eye.

"What?" I whispered. "Jane is my mother. My biological mother. I feel like the plane crash has done something to you. Did you hit your head?" I was so confused.

"Ha ha." She giggled. "No baby, Jane paid me so she could be your mother." She had tears race down her face into the sea, I took her hand off my face.

"What?" I stared at her seriously, still on my back.

"I promise, as soon as we get on land, I will get your birth certificate and prove it."

"I'm so confused, my head hurts. Then why did you give me away? Why Jane?"

"I gave you away because I was only 18. I was broke and I didn't want to kill you because I didn't have the resources. Jane was my friend's cousin and she was 25 at the time and was infertile, so she couldn't have a child. Jane also had money and paid me £2,000 as a thank you. But I regret that so much." She hesitated and there was silence.

"That explains why my sister was adopted, is she your daughter too?"

"No, just you, baby." She kissed my cheek.

"Mum, it was so kind what you did and how considerate you were of giving me a better life, but why do you regret it?" I placed my hand on her cheek, so she felt comforted.

"Because a year later, I met up with my friend and I asked how you were. She said that you were fine, but Jane was abusive towards her husband 'Jaimie', and that she forced him to get a job to leave for a long time which was in 'Photography', but then she started to miss him and became a drug addict to help with the depressed emotions. I stormed out of that café with rage at how big of a mistake I made.

She could have killed you." She hesitated. "Ever since, I have searched the planet to find you, I'm so happy I did." She smiled.

"Oh my gosh, you are my mother!" But then I had to tell her what I had been through. "Um... Mum. There's something I need to tell you." I gulped and looked at the sky. "Jane did try to kill me once. Not long ago actually." I slowly looked up at her face.

"What did you just say?" she said. "When I get on land, I'm killing her!" She punched the water which made a huge splash in my face. It took a few seconds for her breathing to go back to normal. "Oh, baby I'm sorry. I am so protective over you now I have you, I will never let you go, I promise to always keep you safe."

"Don't worry, Mum, I put her in prison, the police took her away and I have stayed with your friend's family for a while, they took great care of me and they have children, so I had a lot of entertainment." I laughed.

"Wait, was her name Rachel?"

"Rachel, yes. She is the greatest. But, why didn't she phone you sooner?"

"After the day at the café, we never spoke again, I blamed Jane being a drug dealer on her. I never got to apologise." She looked to the sky. The fire glistened in her eye, from the plane not so far away.

"You do know that she was on the plane, right?" I tilted my head to the side.

"What?" Suddenly, we both heard a merciful scream of pain.

"Nova! Nova!" That was Rachel, I was so happy to hear her voice (but not like that)!

"Where are you?" I screamed back. "Mum, splash the water." I panicked.

"Of course, yes that's a good idea. By the way, my name is 'Zara', Zara Whittle. But we can catch up later!" Then we saw Rachel paddle over here. This was something out of a horror movie because as I tried to lift my head, I finally saw all of the pleading passengers hanging onto the plane that was on fire to stay alive.

"Rachel," she whispered under her breath.

"Zara."

They swam like athletes towards each other and hugged with tears everywhere; they cried, wiping each other's tears away. Then Rachel came to kiss my forehead as she treaded water. "You are such a hero, Nova. I saw you on the plane screaming, I wanted to unbuckle myself so bad to help you, I couldn't bear it," Rachel cried. "I was so scared; I can't even believe this has just happened." She held my hand floating in the water, I could feel her shaking. As we had been in the ocean for a while, we became warmer.

A few hours later as we all conversed trying to forget where we were or what had just happened, my back started to ache and all I wanted to do was move onto my stomach and curl up, "Mum, my back. I need to move; I feel like it's going to snap," I whined.

"OK, baby calm down, it's going to be OK. But, if you move, you could damage it. So just hang tight. If you want, I can hold it from under the water, for support," she replied. I nodded. As Zara swam to my aid, Rachel knew I knew.

"So, you know. About the mother and adoption." She smiled.

"Ah, yeah. To be honest, I'm really happy. I just can't believe it. I wouldn't change it for the world. Where do you live?" I wondered.

"In Thailand, baby."

"Wait, so am I or not going back to Wales?" I was super confused.

"No, you live here now. But, if you do need anything from your old house, I will send someone over." '...Send someone over'? Why wouldn't she do it herself? Is she rich? Probably not, I'm not that lucky, but I'll leave that conversation for when we're not in the ocean.

Unexpectedly, a miracle happened.

A wealthy man had just been cruising on holiday around the Indian Ocean with his crew for a break and was heading back. He was a very generous man and came closer and closer to us and helped everyone on board his yacht. (Everyone survived the crash, and there were a few with major injuries, including myself.) He placed a metal ladder into the sea to give an easy escape from the ocean's claws.

Then for me and a few others, he dropped in a blanket and with the help of Zara next to me, she placed it under me and used it as a stretcher to haul me out safely. Zara climbed up the ladders as I was being pulled up, so she was with me the whole time, holding my hand. As I was placed very gently onto the sofa, I was very happy; so much that I felt I was dreaming. Then my back had a sharp pain. I screamed in pain, gabbing everyone's attention.

"Isabelle!" Zara screamed in worriedness. "What's wrong? Tell me, baby!" Then she moved the wet blanket from being wrapped around me and then out came a stream of blood, dyeing everything around me blood red. "Oh my god! What do I do?" Then the doctor on board came rushing up the stairs from beneath us.

"Out of my way!" he yelled. He knelt down beside me noticing the blood in horror. "Where does the pain hurt?"

"My back!" I cried.

He asked Zara and Rachel to help him roll me onto my side. "One, two, three." The pain was excruciating. Then everyone saw the large piece of metal pierced through my back. It was from the metal that knocked me as I was in the sky falling. I don't think it hurt because I was in the ocean with adrenaline, coldness and rain distracting me. The doctor was ordering people to collect objects from around the ship that would help.

"Mum, it hurts."

"Baby, you're so brave. Keep going, everything that he's doing is helping, OK?" She smoothed my forehead.

He splashed some cleaning solution for cuts on my back, and it stung like you wouldn't believe. I bit into the sofa for reassurance, squeezing the wet blanket that I laid on.

Then a couple of painful moments later (which felt like hours) the doctor slowly laid me back on my back and the pain was almost gone, it was just a small tingle left.

Everyone walked away leaving me to rest when Zara asked Rachel to get some water so she could talk to me alone.

She sat on the floor with a towel to replace the sea-soaked blanket.

As I got tucked in, she placed her chin on the sofa next to my face and smiled so brightly. "I'm so proud of you. I genuinely can't believe everything that you have gone through. You deserve the world, my darling. I can't explain how happy I am to have found you. I was travelling to Wales on a business trip if you were wondering, but how lucky am I to have found you? Hey?" She held my shivering hand. The rain disappeared and the clouds faintly drifted away. As the sun shone through the glass ceiling, I was relaxed.

"Thank you, Mum." Then I fell asleep out of exhaustion and adrenaline wasting my energy.

A couple hours later, I woke up to the rocking of the yacht like a seesaw. I was still in the same place as when I fell asleep, and as it was dark, everyone was sleeping around on the floor and Zara was still resting her head on the sofa next to me. I sat up and my back was perfect. My eyes widened as I was fully functional. The air was cold and crisp, the vicious waves were thrashing against the boat and the moon was the only natural light that let me see my surroundings.

I slowly swung the towel off me and crept onto the wooden floor towards the stairs leading down into the cabin to find a jacket. I slid open the door and walked down the corridor to a wardrobe built into the wall. I pulled out a drawer from the bottom of the cabinet and there, were all the jumpers and tracksuit bottoms. I quietly knelt down and collected three jumpers and three tracksuits. One set for me and the others for Zara and Rachel. As I stood up, my knees clicked so I tip-toed to the door quickly, but the bedroom door opened with a creak, and there stood the wife of the man who saved us.

She looked tired with her hair in a frizz and dark circles around her squinting eyes.

"What are you doing, sweetie?" She walked up to me.

"I'm so sorry. You can have them back, I shouldn't steal." I handed them back, but she rejected.

"Is it cold up there?"

"Just a little, I mean everyone else is sleeping fine. I think it's just me."

"Just take them all, I'm guessing they're for your family. It's the right thing to do. I'll see you in the morning, OK? You need anything, just knock." She smiled and walked back to her bedroom.

"Thank you," I whispered back. She turned around and gave a thumbs-up. As I walked back, I woke up Zara and Rachel and handed them some clothes.

"Oh, honey thank you. How is your back?" Zara sat up.

"It's perfect. I woke up because I was cold and it didn't hurt, there's zero pain." I pulled the jumper over my head.

"That's amazing, I can't even believe you're real. I really can't, you are literally perfection, the sweetest and most thoughtful person and don't forget that you also indestructible." We laughed quietly; I felt like I was having a sleepover with my friends because it was late, we had jumpers on, and we were laughing.

We all sat on the sofa watching the waves go by, with the towels wrapped around us. The light hitting the peaks of the waves was a pretty sight as well as all of the safe people resting well. I was cuddling into Zara which made me feel at ease and safe. After that I fell asleep, I couldn't help it because I was so relaxed.

The next morning, the sun pierced through my eyelids, waking me up to beautiful sounds of the calm sea and talkative people. Everyone had a plate of food and was sitting on cushions enjoying the sun. I sat up for a minute and just smiled being grateful for my good start to the day, when Zara and Rachel came up the stairs with food for themselves and me.

"Sweetie, you're awake. How was your sleep?" Zara was very energetic.

"Great, it was actually really nice. How was yours?"

"Amazing, thanks to you I wasn't cold. Anyway, here's your food, I got some fruit and porridge to fill you up and keep you healthy." She handed it over to me and sat down.

"Thank you so much. I love food, by the way." I laughed.

"I don't blame you; food can never go wrong."

Rachel was sitting with the baby and its mother. The mother was still in shock and didn't sleep very well, so Rachel was keeping her calm. I asked for some water because my throat was dry, so as Zara went downstairs, you would never guess what happened. Something else went wrong.

CHAPTER 12

As everyone was distracted, my breathing became heavier and heavier. This was when I felt like the world was closing in on me again, when I became claustrophobic. I started to shake, so I put down my food and stood up. I tried to distract myself by walking around but I couldn't. It was like a piece of un-done work in the back of my mind. It was déjà vu all over again. I walked to the back of the ship, where it was quiet. I watched the waves as I stood on the railings off the ground.

"What do I do? It's happening again! I can't breathe." I gripped the handrail so hard that my muscles went numb. "OK, what did I do last time?" I was thinking very hard. "Imagine an island, focus on the sounds and the scenery." I breathed deeply; for a second it worked, but before long I was back to struggling. I was wheezing, desperate for air. I dropped to the floor, hitting my knee on the metal rail. I was helpless to myself. I was battling to sit up. Holding onto the banister, I couldn't even call for help.

"Isabelle!? Isabelle!?" Zara cried. I could hear footsteps moving quick.

"Wait. Isabelle?" Rachel had to bring this up now, didn't she?

"Yes, I named her Isabelle. I mean it's up to her if she wants to change it. But, not now Rachel. I need to find her!" she panicked.

As she ran around the corner and saw me on the ground

hyperventilating, she went white. She raced over and skid on the floor. "Baby, what's wrong?" I couldn't answer. Then when Rachel arrived with the doctor, she knew exactly what was up. But it was much worse than last time. But she didn't know that. I started to turn red, like I was running out of air to breathe.

"Honey, look at me in the eyes and concentrate on my pupils. Look at the textures of my eyes and the colour." She held my hands tight; it wasn't working so the doctor had to cut in.

"Alright, Nova. I'm going to need you to close your eyes and focus on your breathing. Think about your lungs filling with air, emptying and filling again."

Nothing was working, so I opened my eyes and my sight became blurry with the colours mixing, my body was uncontrollably shaking. I felt like the world was caving in on me again, that I was being pushed into a box. Then everyone was fading from my reach, or I thought, but it was just my vision playing tricks. Then, I lost consciousness. This time I wasn't with God, I was an angel floating above the scene with my body in sight. It was very bizarre because I was there but not in my body. I saw Zara, Rachel and the doctor surrounding me with a crowd behind them. But I walked over to Mum and held her arm as she was holding my hand.

"Please come back, baby, I need you. My life isn't complete without you. Please." I was heartbroken.

Then a man came and took her arm and pulled her away to give the doctor some space, but Zara was not having it; I stood by her side. She fought to stay by me, she pushed everyone who tried to pull her away. She pleaded to leave her alone. Rachel walked away with tears in her eyes pushing everyone out of her way because she couldn't watch. Zara was yelling, "Leave me alone! My daughter needs me, please!" It was so hard to watch.

I knew that God was watching, this time I wasn't with her because she wanted me to see what happens when I go, to make me understand that loads of people love me. Many people want me to be in their life, because I make them happy. So, I asked to go back and to just be grateful that I have my real family now.

Then I woke up in a happy state of mind, breathing normally. I was bright red, with a cold body and big eyes. Straight away I leaped onto Zara and embraced her with all my heart. I loved her so much and I didn't even know it. At this point we were unbelievably happy. Zara helped me stand up and we slowly walked over to the sofa to sit down and think about what just happened. I then ate some food, had some water to soothe my dry throat and cuddled with Zara.

Soon after, around ten minutes, we started to see land ahead; we all got really excited. We put on our shoes that had dried overnight in their tumble dryer. Then gathered our dry clothes that we took off last night and put them all into Zara's foldable purse, that was in her huge purse that got wet. Then as we docked, we said our thanks for everyone on board, and our goodbyes to everyone on the plane. Lastly, as I was about to get off, the mother of the baby I saved gave me a huge hug.

"How could I ever repay you?" she worried.

"By being nice and providing help for those who need it." I smiled.

"OK, thank you so much, again." I gave her a hug and headed off down the path.

We arrived at the bottom and found a bench to sit on. Zara ordered a taxi, whilst Rachel and I found a restaurant on our phone to eat at. When Zara was finished, we headed for food down the road.

As we got there, it was so cute and vintage. They had cakes, fudge and chocolates. We had a great laugh and talked about what would happen next. Rachel said that she would get a plane home tomorrow and stay with us for the night; if I was her, I wouldn't go on a plane ever again, but she was a warrior. Then as we finished, we strolled outside to find our "taxi", but you would never guess what was there.

"A LIMO?!" I screamed. "This must have been expensive." I hugged Zara.

"Hey. Never put a price on happiness."

"Lesson learned." We laughed. Then as we jumped inside there were sweets, lemonades and seat massagers. This was a great treat. I just didn't know how she could have afforded it. So, I asked.

"OK, Zara. Tell me, what's your job?" I demanded, tugging her arm.

"If you want to know, you'll find out when we get home." She smiled.

"Is it that good?"

"Just wait, just enjoy the moment, because we all know what taking advantage of time leads to." She hugged me. So, I did. I enjoyed the moment; I ate loads of sweets, drank loads of lemonade and massaged my butt with the chair. It was so luxurious. It took us a while to get home, so we talked and talked before we were all tired again.

After long moments, we arrived at her street; there was a gate with a guard checking who we were – she had ID. Then we made our way to her lengthy driveway, I couldn't even see her house yet, it was covered by trees.

"Are you ready?" She jumped with excitement. We climbed out of the car and she covered my eyes and walked me down the driveway. "One, two... three!" I opened them and I was shocked!

"AHHHH!" I screamed with joy. *She's rich. I knew it.*

A beautiful, modern glass-filled house that overlooked the glistening sea, was in my sight. I ran around her screaming. "This is your house?"

"You haven't even seen the inside yet!" She laughed.

"I can only imagine what the inside looks like!" I laughed with pure joy. Rachel stood in happiness, knowing that I was going to be happy now.

As she reached for the keys in her pocket, I saw the lounge from outside and she had a marble coffee table, with rose-gold placemats and loads of green plants, including aloe vera on the counter.

When we entered, we were greeted with a grand two-way staircase, it felt like it was a princess castle. It was literally paradise. Little did I know she was wealthy! There were designer items everywhere, she had a cinema, proper marble counters and a spa! Even better, she made me my own bedroom! I had a walk-in wardrobe, filled with loads of designer clothes. I even had a fish called Turnip, she said she got it so she wouldn't feel so lonely in the house (even though you can't play with or hug a fish, well, whatever floats your boat). I had everything I could ever dream of. I even had my own bathroom! Wow, God is good.

CHAPTER 13

As time went on and I had a bite to eat, I had to get clean from the blood and sea water, so I did.

I went to shower and to my surprise I had a fully stocked cabinet of products for me to use; I got so excited. As I was getting clean, Zara asked her hair stylist to come over as a surprise for me (she told me in advance not to dry my hair without ruining the surprise). She also ordered frozen yoghurt for us to snack on! How awesome was this?!

Rachel also had a shower and got to borrow some clothes from Zara's wardrobe. She was very grateful and still a bit shaken up from the last couple of days, but I guess I was too.

I think I was in my bathroom for over two hours just trying most things. I wore face masks, I waxed (but stopped after doing a strip on my leg because it was excruciating), and I washed my face with products that had gold in them. Then for the fun part, the clothes. I slipped on my designer slippers and walked out of my bathroom and into my bedroom and just stared at my bed. It was a pod! A light up auto-heating pod! I had swing chairs, climbing walls and even a TV. Then I happily jumped over into my walk-in wardrobe to choose an outfit.

In the end I selected a white strapless sweetheart crochet lace dress, with brown fur cuff boots. As I looked at myself in my full-wall mirror, I just thought, *How did I get here? How am I even this lucky?*

Before I went downstairs to get my hair done, I tested out my climbing wall to see how fun it was. It was awesome! It goes all the way to my celling and at the top is a little ledge where you can relax. So, after that I went downstairs to show my mum what I looked like, and with using all these products, I felt like Gold! I was so fresh and eager to see what their reactions were!

"Mum, how do I look?" I popped out of the corner to the lounge.

"OMG. You look like an angel; you don't know how long I have waited to see you dressed up in the clothes I got you. Nova, you're gorgeous." She smiled and ran over to give me a cuddle.

I got really shy after that because all the hair crew and Rachel were watching. Anyway, a lady called Amira did my hair, she was Zara's best hairdresser. "So, honey, what would you like?" This sentence just got me excited.

"Um... I'll just have the simple beach wave curl in a half up half down, please," I excitedly said, with a jump in my stomach.

"Sure." She was a very pretty girl; it was a pity she wore a lot of make-up.

"So, baby, now I have you all to myself, what do you want to do first? I was thinking, clothes shopping, going to a fancy food place, maybe going on holiday, but on a yacht not a plane?" Zara said, rubbing my arm.

"That sounds nice and all, but I just want to get used to all of this before I start spending your money, I just really want to get to know you first," I replied. I felt bad just spending her money straight away, I don't want to be greedy or be a spoiled brat. Then the doorbell rang, so as she ran to the door, I thought to myself, *I think she's eager to spend money on me, but I just have to stay strong.*

As she happily skipped back to me and handed me her special

flavour yoghurt, she wanted to talk to me about my name.

So, we talked and concluded that I would be called Nova because we both thought it suited me more. Even though Zara hated that Jane named me it and not herself, she just had to get over it. Anyway, my frozen yoghurt was flavoured raspberry, mango and watermelon topped off with sprinkles. This was my dream snack. But, to be able to watch TV, eat frozen yoghurt and have my hair done by my mum's personal hairdresser was a comfort feeling. This was pure luxury.

With my hair and yoghurt finished, Mum and I went on a walk down to the beach nearby (Zara lived in Thailand). It was so pretty, the water was crystal clear, the palm trees were tall and colourful, and the sand was so soft that I felt like I was on the softest sugar you could get.

Soon, there was a sunset overhead full of warm colours which was so aesthetically pleasing. I could see Zara smiling at me as I gazed at the sky in delight. You know when you can just tell when someone's really happy? Well, that was what her face showed me.

But I finally really feel at peace with myself, I know I've said this before and it goes the wrong way straight after, but I just feel like nothing can go wrong right now (mainly because there were two armed bodyguards a few feet behind us) but, just also now that I have my real mum, hairdressers and make-up artists, I just feel like they would protect me if I ever got attacked again, they are those types of people.

Then Zara wanted me to sit down for a chat about how life was going to be. "So, now you live with me and we are together mother and daughter, I am never going to have one day for the rest of my life without seeing you, whether that's in real life or facetime." We giggled. "I will always need to know that you're safe. Therefore, you'll be home-schooled and not leave the house without me coming with you or on my permission. Also, when I can, I'll be home," she ordered.

"Wait, so no more speeches or presentations or detentions or interacting with people?" I excitedly questioned (I'm an introvert). She nodded with a big smile on her face because she knew that I was going to be very happy. "OMG! My life officially can't get any better!" I jumped in the sand waving my arms in the air being totally myself.

Then she stood up and reached for my hands to pull me still. "Some other things too, baby girl, if there is ever a problem you tell me straight away, because I'm here to protect you and want you to have a great life from here on. Also, before I forget, I get to buy you something every single day to catch up from the years missed," Mum neatly said. I stopped spinning and sat back down.

"No, Mum. I feel really spiteful getting all of this. There are some kids out there who have nothing. If you want to get me something, then donate to charities. Don't waste your money one me," I stated seriously, looking into her eyes.

"Have you not seen what you've just gone through? It was unreal! You've been attacked, you've protected a baby whilst being thrown out of a plane that was split in half, you've had a huge sharp piece of metal speared through your back and you have had a breathing issue that caused you to be unconscious. To top it all off, it was in the last couple of weeks, not years, WEEKS! You deserve the world." She hesitated. "Look, I see that you want to help these poor people, which is amazing and so pure of you, but I want you to have something that you want, something that I can give to you for your heroism and bravery. I don't think you understand what you've been through, no adult could have done what you have done, in fact nobody on Earth could have done what you did. Please just let me get you something, well, a lot of things." There was silence, I was just reflecting on everything that I had gone through, I amazed myself.

"Mum?"

"Yeah."

"I've been through more."

"What?"

"Remember I told you that Jane almost killed me?"

"Oh, yeah. I forgot about that. What happened?"

"A couple of weeks ago, when Jane was taken to jail after attacking me on the beach, as we were waiting for the police to arrive, she managed to break free of my uncle's grip and attacked May and Rachel who were protecting me in the back room." She stared at me in horror.

"Did she attack you again?" She tried to keep her cool.

"Well, as I was now vulnerable, she threw me out the window onto bricks. Then ran down the road with me in her arms and tried to take me away. I was so scared, but luckily my uncles caught up along with the policeman. Then I was in the middle of tug-of-war and so I became unconsciousness from exhaustion." Zara stared at the sand with her hands in fists. I held her hands. "Also, after all of this, just before we were leaving to go home, I ran away up a mountain without anybody knowing because I just needed time alone. After hours, I became nauseous, and slipped and tumbled down the mountain and landed on rocks. I put my uncles in the hospital, because they came after me to help." My tears poured out and I placed my head in my hands. When Zara saw I was crying she immediately hugged me for comfort, placing her head on my back.

"Well, you're safe with me forever, OK?" She tried to cheer me up. "Well, lucky for you, you get to attend events with me and meet a lot of people," she replied. My tears dried up and I smiled out of pure excitement.

"Wait, what job do you have? What events do you attend? Why are we so rich?" I got confused.

"Wow, a lot of questions. Well, I am an actress and author. I attend Oscars, red carpets and even talk shows. We're so wealthy because I am a very highly paid actress, because I act in very big films, so when I'm on set you will have to come and do your home-schooling in one of the rooms so, again, I know you're safe," she said.

"Wow! I have a famous mum!" I shouted to the people at the beach. "So, where's the paparazzi?"

"Well, firstly, they don't know where I live, and secondly you can't take photos on this beach, so they would get arrested. Anyway, tell me about your life before I met you, if there is anything good from that wretched person I gave you to," she asked.

"Well, there is nothing to be excited for really..." I explained about my two comas. I told her about helping the homeless people and how Rachel's house got broken into.

"You have such a good, pure heart." Then I became distracted.

Suddenly, a boy ran along the beach in his swim shorts. In my eyes, it went in slow motion; his hair was wet from the salty sea water, his eyes were sparkly caramel and his lips thicker than thin. As he stopped to pick up the Frisbee, his body was something to dream about, with all of those muscles, oh my, I had dreams for days, and his skin tanned to a soft caramel, it looked so smooth. He was perfect. I'm not one to like a guy from his appearance, but I just couldn't stop my mind from thinking in this way.

Unexpectedly, he looked over here and smiled, oh his teeth were so straight and sparkly, my fingers twitched, and cheeks blushed. I have never felt like this for a boy before. (This was way more than the guy in the airport.) Mum stopped talking and looked at what I was looking at and knew exactly what I was thinking, my face just showed it, so to put it in perspective, I think I had my first real crush. No-one in my school ever matched up to my standards, but he did with one glance.

"Babe, are you in focus?" I then quickly zoomed back to Zara and looked at her all clumsily, like I had a love spell on me.

"Yeah, I'm fine. Nothing's happening," I hesitated to say. Zara looked at me with the 'Are you kidding me? You totally like that guy,' face. "What? I promise, nothing is happening," I repeated.

"Let's go and talk to that boy, shall we? He seems nice." She was really pulling my last strings. She knew exactly what was going on, it bugged me.

"NO! How about we go home, yeah? It is getting late, I'm kind of tired." Even though it was only 6pm. Zara stood up and ran over to that boy and started talking. She made it look so easy. This was going downhill, he most likely wasn't interested. So, I quickly scrambled to my feet and ran to the car where our bodyguard was. As the car was unlocked, I jumped in quickly and squeezed into the footwell, so I was out of sight.

"What have I done?" I whispered to myself. "Why am I that obvious?"

I heard footsteps coming in the direction of the car and it sounded like more than one pair of feet. As I heard the door handle being opened, I leaped onto the seat, so it didn't look weird. "Nova, this is Dean," Zara said, grabbing my hand and sliding me out onto the sand again.

"Hey, it's nice to meet you." He had a softly deep voice.

"Hi Dean, I'm Nova, whatever my mum has told you it isn't true," I said, trying not to be awkward.

"So, you're ugly and you don't want friends?" he said, confused, so I was confused.

"What did she tell you, Dean?"

"That you were very beautiful, and you were going through a hard time, so you just want to make new friends."

"Oh yeah, I just want some new people to hang out with, as you can tell."

"Do you want to meet up some time and hang out?" He smiled, there was the smile! The smile that held charm.

"Sure, want to go to the cinema?" I got lost in his caramel eyes, I tried so hard to focus on what he was saying.

"Yeah, great!"

"We can take you, Dean, in the limo if you want," Zara said just in time because I had nothing else to say.

"Perfect, tomorrow if that is OK?" he said.

" Uh-huh," I replied, losing my mind again.

"Thanks. Bye Nova." As he walked away, my heart throbbed knowing that I was going to see him again. I fell back onto the seats and Zara laughed like I was dramatic.

"See, it wasn't that hard. All you have to do is talk to him." She stated moving my feet off her seat.

"You don't understand, it is much easier for the person who doesn't have a crush on someone, to ask them if they want to go on a date with their best friend."

"You don't have to ask them out straight away, all you have to do is talk to them and if they respond back nicely, then you have a keeper and you can build it up from there. If they're rude, then you leave because you've found out how they would treat you. Easy." She reached in her bag for lip gloss.

"Mum, it's not that easy! I don't think you understand. I wish it was easy like that, but I'm an overthinker and always think the worst when it comes to things like this. Anyway, on another note, I wish love was still special and romantic like the old days, I know it's still romantic, but is it special? I don't want to text him, I want to be with him, you know. I want to be asked out in person, not over text," I vented.

"Well, maybe he will ask you out in person. These are what dates are for, to get to know people, maybe tomorrow you can drop hints that you like olden-day love."

"He doesn't think it's a date, all he knows is that I need friends, how depressing is that? He just thinks I'm lonely. He'll never actually want me, for me."

"Nova, if any boy is allowed to go on a date with you, then they're the luckiest boys in the universe."

"But they won't see that. I don't have any special qualities. I'm never going to find love," I mumbled on.

"You have so many qualities. If no boy sees that, then they are so delusional and stupid. You are firstly, gorgeous! Secondly, so smart, you are so brave and funny. It's such a delight to be around you, everyone has said it."

"Everyone who, Mum?" I whined.

"The hair crew, make-up crew, my personal assistant. Most importantly, me. I take up 99% of the opinion. You don't see nearly any of your qualities, do you?"

"No, actually I don't. I think you're being delusional. This is all just lies, anyway mothers have to say all of this."

"Mothers don't have to say anything. It is the true and most special mothers that do, because they see your real beauty, that only pure people see. I wouldn't say it if you didn't have it. But you do, and you're going to wear it like a crown! Do you hear me? Repeat after me, I AM BEAUTIFUL!"

"I am beautiful," I whispered under my breath.

"AGAIN!"

"I am beautiful." I talked at normal volume.

"LOUDER!"

"I AM BEAUTIFUL!" I screamed.

"Yes, Nova. Who's beautiful!?" She smiled.

"ME!" I laughed. I then believed her, partly.

After we had a joyful ride home, Zara asked for our driver to leave us a mile away from home so we could walk and enjoy the weather and scenery; the sunset was upon us and the breeze turned warm as it glided past us.

We walked along a quiet neighbourhood with beautiful modern glass houses, a little smaller than ours, but they all had the perfect view of the beach just opposite, our house was overconcentrated with trees.

I took every breath filling my lungs with fresh new air and smiled every time I saw someone else on the street passing by. I think I was going to enjoy my new chapter to life, this was really my breakthrough.

"So, let's talk about your home schooling and daily routine from now on."

"Sure." Not going to lie, I became really excited as this topic was all about staying home and not having to talk to any other people (I'm extremely anti-social).

"So, I've hired someone to take over the home schooling because I will be busy most of the time, and to add to the excitement, with my new acting role, they've provided me a private room for you to come to work with me and you just hang out until the day has finished."

"Wait! Really? This is so cool. Other than school, what would I do for the whole day?" I was happily intrigued.

"I thought I would be a cool mum, and let you order food to the set for us both, I would let you meet the other actors and even let you online shop from the computer I'm buying for you to put in the room," she replied.

"Thanks, but I can order from my phone. I have my own mini bank account." I didn't want her to buy me anything unnecessary.

"No, silly, if I get you a computer, then I can log onto my account and you can purchase whatever you want with my money." I know she was trying to be kind, but I didn't need all this extra stuff.

"Well, we'll see what happens on the day." I got off the subject.

"Well, when we arrive home, I have a surprise for you." She hugged me sideways.

"Mum! Stop with the surprises." I laughed.

"Fine, but last surprise for a while, OK?" she argued.

For the rest of the minutes left walking home, the dark sky was looming around the sun ready to set over us like a blanket, so as we made it to the front door, Zara rushed me upstairs to go and see the surprise.

We entered her two-storey bedroom and climbed the ladder to her secret hideout. "What have you got me?" I said, struggling to climb the awkward ladder.

"OK, sit down and close your eyes." I crawled on the floor and sat on the large white, soft bean bag.

"OK, here it is." It felt large, so I opened my eyes and in front of me was a red, velvet box. I slid off the lid and softly tore the tissue paper. Inside to my amazement, I found a folded ombre yellow and orange dress, with the chest full of real diamonds accompanied with a long trail. My jaw dropped. "Oh my gosh..." I just stared at it. It was just like the dress I adored in the shopping centre with Jane. "Thank you so much, Mum." I wasn't even mad about it.

"I thought you could wear it to our first red carpet." I felt pure anxiety as she announced this to me.

"Red carpet?" I never wanted her to say this, it is my worst nightmare to be photographed by so many people at once and then interviewed straight after. I don't even have a good photogenic face.

"Yes, and you'll be great. You won't have to speak to anyone, all you would have to do is smile, and luckily for you, you have a great smile. I thought I would surprise the world that I have a daughter, and it would be the best way to introduce you."

"Mum, this is giving me way too much anxiety. I can't do this; do you know how fast I would start sweating as soon as I would step out of the car?"

"Baby, I would be with you the whole time. Besides, I think it would really help with your confidence," she reassured.

"You don't understand how nervous I get. Even with ordering a drink in a café, I would start to sweat and shake. This is far too out of my comfort zone."

"Just remember that every celebrity there, would be a little nervous about something. Once they know that you're my daughter, they'll all want to talk to you. Just pretend that you're here to make new friends and enjoy yourself, like a huge party."

"Why would they only want to get to know me if I'm your daughter? As if I'm nothing without you."

"That's not what I meant. I meant that everyone's there for a reason, so they'll be interested in why you're there, and will want to have conversations to get to know you."

"I'll just follow you around and hope for the best."

"Well, that's a better attitude. You never know, maybe you can do something with this and get your name out there." I shrugged my shoulders at this comment, I just wanted to get settled in first, not go to award shows, I mean I literally just met my real mum, can't I just have a couple of days with her?

For the rest of the evening, I just watched movies and ate pizza with Mum; to get the anxiety off my mind. I mean, at least I had a gorgeous dress to wear, although I hope it doesn't draw too much attention to myself.

CHAPTER 14

As I opened my eyes to my luxurious room, there was a glimpse of the sparkling sun emerging from my window that squeezed through the gaps of the trees. I flung my silk sleeping mask across the room and sat up against my headboard and rubbed my feet on the silk bedding.

I didn't think of my date with my dream boy straight away, I just thought about how fortunate I was to be able to have this lifestyle and wake up in the most beautiful room. No matter how much I say it, it will never sink in how lucky I have become. I reached over to my marble and rose-gold bed stand and looked at the time. It was almost mid-day. I wondered why Zara didn't wake me up, so I scrambled out of bed and as my feet touched my luxurious faux fur carpet, I just wanted to stand there all day, my feet were in feet heaven. But I carried on walking into my bathroom to use my hundred thousand skin and body products that were waiting for me.

I had a shower and remembered not to dry my hair because now I have my own hair and make-up crew; yes, I was grateful for them, but I did have to get used to it. Anyway, as I dried off, I strolled on into my walk-in wardrobe and there in front of me was a manikin, wearing an outfit with a letter stuck on the chest.

Dear Nova,

I don't want you to get overwhelmed with your new life and all these presents. But you are my baby and I just want to spoil you because you are gorgeous and perfect. Life is going to be very busy from now on, but I will always be with you. I wanted to give you this as a thank you gift, for being the best child and trusting and accepting that I'm your mum.

Love you, baby x

P.S – this outfit is for your date.

So, now I guess I don't have to find an outfit because she already bought me one, I'm not surprised. This outfit was a white lace blouse with crystals on the shoulders along with a light blue skirt that was down to my ankles and could easily fly in the wind. For the shoes she found a pair of white heels that don't cover the top of your feet. The accessory was a diamond dog necklace that had sea blue eyes. Everything was really comfy, including the shoes (I never wear heels so this was a one-off).

As everything was done from neck to toe, it was time for the hair. With my hair still wet I made my way down the two-way stairs (I always went down the left side).

I approached the beauty room around the corner, and I saw Mum sitting in the chair laughing at a joke that Amira said. I came through the doorway and everyone turned around and stared in delight, making unnecessary sound effects trying to make me feel cute. As Zara turned around, she left her chair and gave me a big hug and forehead kiss.

"You read the letter!" she assumed.

"I did," I hesitated. "It was really nice of you to get me a new outfit. So, am I late for my date?" I questioned because we were supposed to have left an hour ago.

"Oh, no honey you are perfectly fine with the time because I asked Dean if we could move the time until later, because I knew you would love your bed. I customised it to make you have a better sleep because if my life was busy, so would yours be. So basically, I'm happy you've slept in," she stated with grace.

My face lit up that she was so considerate of me and that she knew the struggle of crawling out of a comfy bed. Zara held my hand and dragged me over to my very own chair, called the throne. Today I asked for a very high ponytail with a bunch of hair wrapped around the bobble, because it's very neat for this occasion and because I had a couple of split ends that Amira offered to cut off.

Also, I was getting my make-up done today, by a lady called Valerie. She was a very pretty girl and had a lot of experience with make-up. I just had the casual, natural look with nude lips and dark mascara, no foundation or anything too covering. As I was done, Zara called me to the transport outside which was a WHITE limo! Inside were drinks, snacks and TVs for us to binge watch our favourite shows, even though we wouldn't be in the car for over an hour.

As I climbed inside, Zara followed and sat on the seat opposite, then we started driving and it was paradise. The only thing that bothered me was that Zara went straight on her phone. I know it was work but she had a personal assistant, I just wanted to talk to her about what to say and do without being awkward. The driver was very sweet and was also a great driver, I mean we had a few tight roads! Anyway, as we arrived at Dean's house, he was waiting right outside with herds of paparazzi waiting to take photos; this gave me real anxiety and a little hint of the Red Carpet, but also, how do they know where Zara is?

Zara ordered me to stay in the car and wait until they came back; she was going to talk to his mother before we left, just so Zara knew his mother knew. I found that very responsible.

With my phone I downloaded Instagram and made an account. My name was 'NovaWhittle'. I called it this just in case anyone was suspicious if I was Zara Whittle's daughter. I took a picture of the inside of the limo and captioned it 'How did my life get this good?' with a black and white filter. I posted it because I want to see how many likes it would get if no one knew who I was, then I would see how many likes after The Award Show to see the real impact of fame. I switched off my phone as they ran through the paparazzi. I hid right at the back, so they wouldn't know that I was there.

As Dean climbed in, we smiled at each other as he saw me hiding on the back seat, crouching down. "What are you doing?" He laughed.

"They don't know I exist, so I'm hiding. But, don't make it obvious that I'm here." I laughed.

As Zara closed the door, I sat up and he moved right next me, this made me have butterflies. Our knees and shoulders were touching, but our faces were turned away from each other because it was too awkward to say anything other than, "The weather is nice," which is so cliché.

Opposite us was Zara, on her phone to her manager about hiring the room for me. Mum was writing everything down on her notepad that she needed to remember; her schedule was packed, which meant mine was too!

"So, what film do you want to watch?" I asked, being very impatient towards the silence, turning my body towards him.

"You know, I feel like an Action movie. I have been really into those lately," he replied. I nodded and looked back out the window, trying very hard to think of the next question. Then out of nowhere he made a conversation. "I would've never guessed that your mum was famous." Zara looked up at him, then me.

"Actually, I didn't either."

"What?"

"I just met her."

"I'm so sorry, what?" Oh, here we go...

CHAPTER 15

"Long story short, when she was eighteen, she gave me away to a lady. Then she realised she made a mistake; she's been looking for me for over a decade. Then we met me on a plane a couple of days ago. Found out that she was my mum and found out that she was famous. Here we are, in a limo."

"I did not expect that." He laughed. "You are very lucky."

Then Zara came off the phone and added herself to the conversation. "Well, she is very lucky. But, she's a strange one because she doesn't want anything off me. She just wants to donate it all to charity, which isn't bad at all, it's just I thought that I want to get her gifts from all of the birthdays and Christmases missed from over the years, but she isn't having it."

"Thanks Mum." I was annoyed at her saying I was 'a strange one'. Just because I want to give it all to charity doesn't mean I'm weird.

"No, I think it's nice that you want to give it all to charity. I mean, I don't know many people who would come into this wealthy lifestyle, where you have the choice of getting anything you want, and donate it all to charity. I think it's cute," Dean added. This made me feel like I was in a dream, a boy talking nice to me, calling me 'cute'. OMG.

Then we were interrupted. "Here we are, everyone, I'll be back in two hours," Bob stated. He pulled himself out of the car and like a gentleman he opened the limo door for us to enter the cinema (he parked around the back where no paparazzi were allowed, to help hide me). I got out and Dean was right behind.

"Guys, I am going shopping now," Zara shouted out the car. "Text me if you need anything." Then the car door shut, and we headed up the back stairs being escorted by a member of staff.

"This is so exciting; it feels like we're in VIP." He jumped. "I haven't been to the cinema in years. What about you?" He got interested.

"I have never been to the cinema before." Looking at my surroundings and the film covers on the walls. "I am very excited." I clapped my hands together.

As we got to the till, we had £50 to spend from Zara beforehand in cash (which in Thailand was 2026.59 Thai baht), I know looking back it is a lot, but I didn't really know at the time because I thought the cinema was expensive, considering I've never been before. Nevertheless, we bought our tickets. Adding to our items, we purchased some ice cream (cookie dough), and a large popcorn with some gummy sweets because Dean was obsessed. As we headed in, we looked around for seats g16 and g17. Then we reached our lettered row and sunk into the comfiest numbered seats. That day the cinema was totally empty, no-one was there other than a lady all by herself who sat right at the front. We on the other hand were alone.

The advert appeared and made me jump with the volume of sound and bright colours. I felt alive. Dean sniggered as I jumped as he went in for some treats. "Shut up." I shoved him.

"I'm sorry, I've never been with someone so frightened of the cinema screen." He sniggered some more.

"Why didn't you tell me it was going to be so loud?" I laughed.

"I'm not used to telling my friends to be cautious of the cinema screening because of the noise." Yes, you guessed it, he sniggered some more. I shoved him again, laughing along.

Then as the film actually started, we sat back and relaxed. Five minutes in I went for some popcorn and as I was exiting the tub, Dean went for some and we made contact. My heart froze. I swear I was not concentrating on anything other than what just happened. I did not move, neither did he.

All of a sudden, he dropped his popcorn back into the box and slid his hand into mine. That meant I dropped all of my snack too. I have to be honest; it was not the most romantic "hand hold" that I would have imagined, only because it was gritty from the popcorn residue left on our hands. I just tried to ignore that bitty feeling and leant over and rested my head on his shoulder; my heart was pumping out of my chest.

We held hands for the whole film and close to the end he started to smooth his hand over my forehead, like my dad used to do when I was miserable. I loved it and almost fell asleep. As soon as the end credits were showing, the lights flickered on and we let go of our hands, I picked up our rubbish and placed it onto our seats for the cleaner. I wanted to take it out to the bin, but Dean says that is what everyone does. I'm no sheep, but I was sleepy after the film, so I just followed what he did.

"Did you like the movie?" he asked as we headed to the front door.

"It was good, but I didn't like how they started the film, they really need to upgrade their disguises."

"I know, right! I guess it's just traditional."

"Yeah. Well, we have time to get some real food. Where do you want to go?"

"Anywhere, but won't paparazzi recognise me? From coming out of my house before the cinema."

"No, they would have followed my mum somewhere else. But, just to be safe, let's put our jacket hoods up and walk straight into a café."

CHAPTER 16

A couple minutes across the street, we found a modern café that sold some healthy nutritious food. We sat at the back as far away from the window as possible. Having some money left over from the cinema, we ordered some pasta and smoothies. Yes, very filling, but we were hungry after the long film.

"So, I want to get to know you more. What was your life like before you met Zara?" he asked, taking a spoonful of cheesy pasta.

"I don't know if you're ready."

"Why?"

"Because a lot has happened, I have had many near-death experiences."

"Woah, tell me more." I was surprised, I thought he would say something like, 'Tell me if you want, you don't have to.'

Anyway, "Before my life was crazy, I have had two comas, I have met God, I have been assaulted twice by my fake mother that Zara gave me to. I have recently been having breathing issues that have caused me once to go unconscious. I have tumbled down a mountain and landed on rocks, I was also in a plane crash, saved a baby's life and harmed many other people in the process. I haven't been physical to them, but they have been put in hospital. With me being a mess, I've caused other people's lives to be damaged." I paused.

"What? No offense but how aren't you dead?" He hesitated,

realising that hurt me. "I'm sorry. You are so brave. Are you OK now?" He became concerned.

"Yeah." He held my hand. "I'm actually perfect now. I went from hell to heaven, after finding out my real mum is rich and famous and mostly kind, to meeting you." It became cheesy fast.

"Thanks. You are amazing. But I cannot believe your life was like this and you are still in one piece, I'm very proud." Then we ate and chatted about his life and even more about mine. His life as he told me was also a mess. Dean's mum lost her job years ago and they became homeless until their uncle let them move in. They still don't have that much money but are very happy now and that made me excited to bring him into my new extraordinary life that he could share with me.

"So, by you being part of my life it is going to get hectic. Tomorrow I have a red carpet to go to. A whole award show! I am super nervous, so can you be here tomorrow morning to keep me calm to get ready?" I anxiously asked.

"I might be a bit late, but I will try." I was grateful for his effort.

"I just want to spend a lot of time with you because I have no friends as I'm starting fresh," I stated which was quite depressing, but I needed to get it out of me.

"I know what you mean, don't worry. I will always be here for you from now on!" I found this statement quite endearing. I felt safe with him; my mind was a bit confused by how much I had attached myself to him so quickly.

As we finished with our food, we headed out to walk along the wide lake. It was a beautiful sky, with no clouds to be seen, just pure blue! There were even palm trees along the street, I felt like I was in Hollywood almost. We saw a bench far ahead that we headed to.

"Nova I have had the best day today. I cannot thank you enough because you show me that there is always light at the end of the tunnel. So, I wanted to ask you something that I'm going to find hard to say." He became very nervous.

CHAPTER 17

My heart rate rose. "I promise I won't laugh or overreact at whatever you are going to say. Don't be nervous, I'm here for you." I rubbed his shoulder and smiled so he would not feel intimidated.

"OK, thanks," he said. Dean looked into my eyes; all I could see was the sun glistening on the pupils.

"Yeah. Just say it like ripping off a bandage. That's what I do." At this point I had no idea what he was going to say. This could go two ways. I was only hoping it would be good.

"Will you be my girlfriend?" he said gracefully. Hoping that I would say 'yes'.

"Of course! Yes!" I hugged him so tight. A big cheesy grin appeared on my face because I was so delighted.

As we let go, I got out my phone and took a picture of us to capture this moment. A few minutes passed and I got a call from Zara to tell her where we were so they could pick us up. We were so spoilt. But then I said we would meet them behind the cinema just in case paparazzi were following them.

As we arrived, they were already there. We jumped inside, and just my luck it started to rain. Zara had bags full of items at the back.

"Well, you did well with shopping." I laughed.

"Thanks for reminding me. Dean, I have something for you." She slid over the seats to the back and reached in, searching for something.

"You really didn't have to get me anything, Zara," Dean said.

"Yeah, but you have been so kind to my daughter. I have not seen her this happy since I have met her. So, you deserve at least something little." She pulled out a small box and sat back opposite us and handed it over.

As Dean opened it up, he gasped to his delight. It was a £60,000 designer watch. "Oh, Zara you didn't!" Dean teared up. "It has been my actual dream to own one of these, you're such a blessing." He leant over and gave Zara an enormous hug.

"Oh, it's nothing. You're part of the family now." She smiled.

"Wow, Mum that is generous." I like people to get along, but to be part of the family is too far. What happens if I do not end up liking him? I do not want him taking my mum's money for just being nice to me, I would rather that I got him something. Some would say this is jealous, I'm saying it as being protective over my mother.

As we reached his house, I rushed him out so I could talk to Zara.

"Bye Nova, I've really enjoyed today."

"OK, bye." I slammed the door. To be honest, I have no clue of what just came over me, I shouldn't have been that impolite, I could tell that he wanted to talk.

"Don't be so rude, Nova. Don't slam a door in someone's face like that." She became frustrated. Was this the first time she would tell me off? Who knows?

"Bob, let's go!" I ordered.

"NOVA!" she yelled. This brought me back down to earth.

"What were you thinking?" I whispered back.

"What are you on about?"

"Buying my boyfriend a £60,000 watch?" (This whole

conversation was in whisper mode.)

"I was just being nice."

"You're throwing money out the window, on someone that we just met. For all we know, he is just with me for your money. Stop giving him what he wants." I got angry. "You know what?"

"What?"

"I would rather you buy me things than him." I hesitated. "From now on, only buy me things!"

"Wait! Really?" She became happy and excited. I just rolled my eyes.

I brought out my phone and went onto Instagram and looked at likes and how many followers I got. For that one picture of the limo, I gathered eighty likes and twenty followers. I was impressed. I scrolled to the comments and read the first comment. It read, 'Is your mum Zara Whittle?' I felt sick. I turned it straight off.

"So, tell me what happened," Zara asked, sliding across the long seat to me.

"Well, all I can say is we are together now." That made Zara very excited. As I got in the house, I ran up to my room because I was frustrated, and I just needed to sleep.

CHAPTER 18

In the morning, I woke up to the sound of chatter downstairs, then I remembered it was the day of the award show. I was very shocked to learn how many people we needed. So, I popped in the shower for a quick wake up.

I walked down the stairs in a robe and (faux) fur slippers.

As time went by, I ate some mango for breakfast while having my hair done by Amira in a space bun with swirly-whirly strands of hair hanging down. After, I walked upstairs into my wardrobe and saw my diamond ombre dress waiting to be worn. I called down to Zara to ask if she could help me put it on because it was a crazy large dress.

Not to brag, but I felt flawless, I had never felt more like a princess in all my life. It's crazy how a dress makes you feel so special. So, I gracefully strolled downstairs with my train gliding behind me, with my crystals glistening in the chandelier light. I reached the bottom of the stairs and the mirror wall really reflected the dress's beauty. The beauty crew were waiting in the kitchen for me, and as they saw me walk past, they walked behind complimenting how gorgeous I was. I really did feel like someone in this moment.

Then I sat in my throne and had my makeup done. I was not extremely happy about having my make-up done, but Zara just wanted me to fully experience the event and make me feel great. I also received a phone call ten minutes in from Dean, saying that he was going to be late. I was not mad because he did say this yesterday in the café.

An hour or so later, Dean arrived at the house but went straight to the toilet. So, I stayed on my phone scrolling and searching for past award shows that Zara has been in, only because during my make-up process, I had not glanced into the mirror because I wanted a before and after, not a step by step. When Dean came back, he sat in the other chair chatting to me about his life and telling jokes, because I had asked him to distract me.

When I was finished, Dean had to take a phone call outside with his mother. So, I took a deep breath and gazed into the mirror reflecting my different face.

I did not recognise myself. My eyes dropped to my lap. I thought this would be a new change for me, something I would like, but I could not stand to look in the mirror and see a better-looking person than me. I wanted to arrive to the award show looking like myself to see if people actually wanted to talk to me about my own beauty. That is what I hate about make-up, it makes you look different, it hides your own natural beauty that you were born with. (I know you don't buy make-up to look the same, but no-one actually needs it. Society these days has a huge impact on girls and some boys to look a certain way to fit in. But, please don't fit in!)

Even though I didn't fully love my face for what it was, I didn't want to hide it and become a different person to trick other people of what I actually looked like. Yes, from time to time I put on mascara, apply a layer of gloss, but never a full face. I didn't like it. *At least I will look photogenic now?* I thought. *Oh who am I kidding? I hate it!*

As I hurled the towels off my lap (that were protecting my dress), I shot out of the chair and darted upstairs. In the process I dropped my phone on the marble floor and it smashed, not cracked, SMASHED into thousands of pieces, I was that confused! As I flew into my bedroom, I slammed my door shut and locked it (by saying 'locked it' I mean placing my dresser in front of it). In my bathroom there was a window that could lead to the roof. Bearing in mind, I still had my massively long, heavy diamond dress on, and skinny high heels underneath. Basically, saying I had completely forgotten what I was wearing and was about to, again, make another absurd decision.

I hesitated at the thought of climbing to the roof for some privacy. But I heard footsteps galloping up the stairs after me, with the sound of my name firing through the door like gun shots, so I began the climb from my bathroom. I ran to open my window (without locking the bathroom door behind) tripping over my dress once or twice, which did make me think, *Should I take it off?* but with the banging of fists on my bedroom door, I had no time to think. I flipped the lock off the hatch and opened the large square window that filled the wall. I took a deep breath and pivoted my leg up onto the windowsill and managed to pull myself up. Then looking over the ledge, it was a high drop.

I suddenly heard my door handle squeak, like in the horror movies. In a panic and risen heartbeat, I draped over the edge of my windowsill and stared at the ground (it didn't even look this high when I was on the ground level). Anyway, you know when you want to move, but you're so scared you physically can't? Yeah, this is what my body was going through. I just had faith and placed a good grip on the brick outside, with my other hand holding onto the stones on my bathroom wall. I shakily moved my high-heeled shoe outside onto the wall; I felt so unstable, I didn't trust my foot at all to hold my body weight. I just had to keep going.

"Nova come out, baby! Whatever is wrong we can talk about it. If it's about your phone, I'll buy you a new one right now!" Zara cried as she thrashed against the door. As she hit again, she injured her wrist, I remember her scream in pain.

"It's probably just a trick," I whispered to myself as I rolled my eyes. Blindly, I was trying to find a good foot hole, I was dragging my foot up and down the wall until I found one that I could trust. After a couple of trembly moments, I rested my foot on a stable brick. But this is where I went wrong. You can't rush in these moments, but with the sound of my cabinet moving on the carpet in my room (that helped keep the door locked), it scared me into letting go of the stone wall in the bathroom, and so, with a stupid action comes a huge consequence. I slipped.

"Ahhh!" I screamed. My right hand was dangling beside me and in this moment, all I had was one foot steady and a weakening left hand with fingers going white. I did not find a good brick to grab onto for my right hand, and with the weight and length of my dress I couldn't find another foot hole whilst being heavily weighted down to earth. In this process, the right hand decided to reach across me and grasp onto the window handle. With my desperation being filtered all through my body, I pulled too hard on the window, forcing the latch to snap off the wall (holding the window in place) and so, the window flew towards me.

The window handle was on the inside, so as it flew towards me, my body was propelled outwards, now even more vulnerable to fall. (If you need help imagining it, I'm in an abseiling position, just not attached to anything and my hand was twisted.) As my hand on the brick was getting sweaty and achy, I had to get another grip before I would fall.

As I pivoted my head to my right, I saw that the pool was not that far away behind me, so I very slowly moved right feeling for something to grip whilst taking deep breaths and letting out little whines as I scratched my arms on the rough wall. I suddenly panicked again, with a rush flowing through my heart, so I grabbed the gutter, that was a hundred percent not sturdy! As I was stuck in this situation, all I could hear was my heart beating and my breathing. I thought about all the situations that could take place in these very next moments.

I just whispered, "Even though you might break something by jumping, you'll be a lot smarter if you don't stay here any longer because you won't have any power to push off the wall into the pool, so you could die if you don't jump now." I had to do it, what other choice did I have? I heard my bedroom door open; I couldn't see anybody because I was away from my window. Then all of a sudden, a head peeked out from my bathroom, it was Amira.

"Nova!" she screamed. "Zara, she's hanging off the wall!" She ran back inside, and I could hear her ordering everyone downstairs and into the back garden. Then Zara peeked her head out. Her face became a piece of paper.

"Baby! What are you doing?!" She stuck her hand down the wall to try and reach me. "Baby take my hand; I can help you. Please do not do this. You mean the world to me, we can work things out, I promise."

I ignored her and tried to think straight, but every moment wasted my muscles were weakening, all I could hear were the screams of Zara and the crowd beneath me. It was now or never. I closed my eyes and pushed as hard as I could off the wall, screaming in the process.

When I was in the air, I felt that time had paused. I saw my long-layered dress flow in front of me, my shoes above my body and my hair fluttering right next to my ears, I could see Zara's face terrorised, with her hand in the air reaching for me, screaming. Do you ever have those moments where things happen so fast, but you can remember a certain facial expression that someone made, and you keep picturing it in your head over a thousand times?

Soon after I flew through the air, I landed headfirst into the pool, and with the concrete hardness of the water from a large height, my neck felt like it had snapped as it made the connection, and with the pressure affecting my ears, it made them pop as I sunk to the deepest depth of the pool. The item keeping me at the bottom of the pool was my weighty dress; I was covered by my dress like it was protecting me, almost like a bubble. As I looked at my skin, tiny air pockets appeared and then were whisked away by my soft hair swimming around me, it was almost like a sign to push off the ground and swim for safety, but I felt paralysed and numb. My vision started to cloud over as I lay on the ground looking upwards, the bright lights became smudges, the sounds were silent as you cannot hear under water; it felt as I was in the ocean because the bottom was murky. My neck hurt and I became desperate for air, but if you looked at me, you would have thought that I was not bothered at all, but I was. I felt trapped inside of somebody else's body.

Suddenly on the surface, faces appeared, wobbling faces. I could not make out their facial expressions, but I would have thought that they were strained. As I laid there, I felt like dissolved sugar in tea, as I saw the make-up float off my face. I was not too mad about this, I was happy to get it off, but maybe next time, in my bathroom with soap and water.

As my lungs ran out of air, and I saw the last bubble spill from my mouth, an arm shot through the water. It felt like a heroic moment for this person, the human (or I hope it was) captured my arm and pulled me upright. I had no feeling in any part of my body, so the human held up my head (bearing in mind I could not see) and just looked me in the eyes and could see my lifeless face, growing paler and paler. Let me be honest, I don't think this person knew how long I was under there for, so this whole "heroic movie" scene was not helping to save my life by just staring me in the eye and hoping for the best. As they finally pushed their feet off the base of the pool whilst I was being cradled in their arms, I passed out for literally two seconds.

CHAPTER 19

As soon as the air hit my lips, I gagged on the water trying to steal my breath and was sick all over my hero. As I could now see it was a man, I started to hallucinate as the air was slowly getting back to my brain, and a thought popped up in my mind that it was, "DAD?" My voice strained.

I squinted into his eyes and tried to sit up as I clung onto his arm; this man could have been anyone, I think at this point I would have let anyone be my dad because my life has been so messed up. But I didn't have the strength to keep my eyes open, so I fell onto the pavement tiles around our pool and injured my head with a sharp pain, but lucky for me I didn't feel a thing, I was just told this.

When I woke up (couple hours later as I was told, again), I was clean (Amira and Zara washed me before Zara left for the Award Show) and in my bed with the silk sheets and fluffy blankets. It was late at night, but as I rose to check the time, I noticed that the man who saved me, was in my room sleeping on my swing chair. I've got to say he looked very peaceful. I crawled out of bed with my silk night-gown trailing behind, I sat at the end of my bed, with my legs dangling off and my arms holding me up beside me. I watched him sleep for a period of time before I ambled over to the swing-chair to hold his hand.

I sat on the floor on my knees and my head resting on his knee and said, "Thank you, stranger." I rose quietly from the floor, and decided to walk over into my bathroom and to write a note.

Dear Stranger,

I have no clue who you are, but I just wanted to say thank you. Thank you for saving my life. I can't tell you how very grateful I am, I wasn't thinking clearly when I jumped off the wall, I will never know why I couldn't just sit in my room to have privacy, but I was so stupid doing what I did. The lesson I learned from this, is if I died, I would have created more trauma and sadness for my family than for me, just to do something for myself, which would've been selfish. But There is one more thing I have to say, I am so new to this amazing lifestyle, that I am lost and scared. I went from no one wanting to even look at me to I cannot go outside without hiding from people.

With everything going on and everything I have and getting from Zara, it is too much, I know she loves me, and I love her, but I don't need it. Just to let you know, it is 1:30 a.m. and I'm leaving to go back to Australia. I am going back because most of my true, but nonrelated family is there and for me it's the perfect lifestyle, no assistants or paparazzi.

If you are more to me than just a saviour, maybe my father, you will come after me and tell me who you are. Show this to Zara if you want to, but I am basically saying goodbye. Forever.

Yours Sincerely,

Nova x

I tucked the paper in his pocket and walked to my wardrobe to start packing. At this moment Zara was at the Award Show, so it was just me and the stranger, or I thought it was. I grabbed my designer luggage suitcase and zipped it open. I was surrounded by millions of shoes, bags, accessories and clothes. So, I started at the clothes, then shoes and so on. I was basically in a dream. Now don't get me wrong, there are some perks of being rich, for example having really fashionable clothes. Yes, there are nice cheap clothes, but can you even compare them to the extravagant ones?

During this process I kept checking on the person in my room to see if he was awake. I was very quiet and even a bit cheeky because I went into Zara's room and "borrowed" £10,000 just to cover my travels. I only did this because she was rich, I wouldn't ever do it to someone if they were not a mega-rich human. Besides, Zara would be happy for me to take anything off her right now. I stuck this in my expensive purse and stuck that into my expensive suitcase, just in case someone would find out that I took it, and especially for good security. I then cautiously walked into my bathroom to pack my cosmetics and beauty products.

As I wandered back into the wardrobe, I went to close my door and Pasher, my other hairdresser, was standing in plain sight.

I jumped out of my skin and fell into my open wardrobe backwards. "Shhhhh! Don't scream, can we just talk?" he whispered.

"No! Go away, can't you see I'm doing something?" I argued. Now, I'm not rude or anything like that, but when I'm trying to escape from anything, I would rather not be interrupted. Pasher tip-toed in and closed the door.

"What are you doing?" He became interrogative and tilted his head.

"None of your concern, so please go away." I started to get annoyed.

"Well it looks to be my concern, and why at 2 a.m.?" (Yes, Zara was late coming home, but she loved to stay until at least three in the morning to celebrate with her other friends, since this is a once-a-year thing) Pasher started to become sassy. No offence to Amira but, I prefer him because he's quite funny and entertaining to be around.

"If I tell you, will you leave me alone?" To be honest I was quite cranky because it was early, and I am not a morning person by far.

"Maybe."

"No, you have to promise so I can trust you. By the way, what are you doing here so late, aren't you supposed to be at your house?" I got off topic.

"Fine, I promise! Anyway, Zara told me to stay here all night because she wanted me to make sure you were safe, she doesn't fully trust that man."

"You don't know this man either?"

"I'll tell you later."

"Anyway, I am going back to Australia because I don't like it here. This lifestyle is too much for me. I have loads of kind people back in Australia that are literally family to me, so I can be myself, without all this paparazzi, make-up and hair every – single – day. No offense. Don't tell Zara, but I'm leaving tonight, and you can't stop me." I saw Pasher's face and it did not look good.

"WHAT?!" he silently yelled. "We all love you here. I know it's a big change, but give us another chance please, we'll make it better I promise." He looked me in the eye with desperateness.

"Why do you love me? You don't know me. All I give to you is orders, I bet Zara has paid you to say this." Pasher frowned his eyebrows as if to say, 'Are you serious?' I sighed. "Anyway, I am never nice to you; I feel so selfish. You should be happy anyway because I'm giving you less to do. Because I'm leaving." I sat on the floor in misery, piling clothes into my suitcase. Pasher sat next to me and hugged me with his right arm. We sat there for a few seconds in silence staring at the mess I had created.

"We love you because you are family. Zara never stopped talking about you for five whole years once she hired me. When you arrived, you were an angel. We saw from the start you were nervous, all we wanted to do was make you feel at home, that's why she showered you with gifts. No matter how mean you would be to us, no matter how many orders you would give us, we would know that it was because you were new and anxious." He squeezed my shoulders.

"Thank you. But I still want to leave because I'm scared, of my security and all of these new people. When I was in Wales with Jane, I got so anxious from asking someone at the food shop where the flour was, but now I have to be around crowds of people daily and talk to them, that's a huge ask from me." I thought of an idea — because I'm afraid of travelling on my own, why not bring Pasher? "Um... since I really trust you and you say that you love me, will you go to Australia with me?" I felt so much better after hearing what he said, but I was nervous that he would say no and stop me from leaving because he cared about me too much. I clutched my cosmetic bag with sweaty palms awaiting his answer.

He hesitated; I could see him really think of the best option. "Fine, I'll come. But only because I love you and want to keep you safe, I could never live with myself if something happened to you and I could have stopped it. Besides, this can be our first adventure together." I was so ecstatic that Pasher said yes that I quietly jumped in the air.

We gave each other a huge hug. I soon realised that the man was still in my room, so I told Pasher that we had to leave quickly.

A few moments later I had gathered my suitcases and dragged them onto the landing next to our sitting area, after I locked my bedroom door to keep the man from catching us if he did wake up. I needed a sit-down break from everything that I had packed and from how fast I did it. Normally I am a light traveller, but since I had been given designer everything, I had to give some to my cousins when I got back to Australia, so I packed extra. I sat on the Cloud Couch, as we call it, because it feels as if you are sitting on a cloud in heaven, and slid my phone out of my pocket. I phoned the taxi company to take us to the airport. The only reason why I didn't hire a limo or anything else fancy, was because I didn't want to draw attention or be suspicious if Zara did drive past. As I came off the phone from talking to the woman who said that she would be here in five minutes (she had just dropped off people down the road) Pasher came out with his luggage from the downstairs kitchen and walked upstairs to me. All he had was what he brought over this morning, it was only what was in his bag, so no clothes. He sat down next to me and took and deep breath.

"You ready? You sure you want to leave? Zara will be—"

"I know. Sad. But it's my life and I can't live with paparazzi and assistants for everything I do, every single day of my life. I don't need it, I'm independent and Zara can come after me if she really wants me. Now let's go before I get a mental breakdown." You see the little things in life really get me down, quickly, especially if people know how I feel about something, but they still ask. As we stood up, carried our luggage downstairs, slid on our shoes and went to go grab a snack from the pantry for our journey, it was kind of awkward.

On our way, I couldn't stop saying sorry to Pasher, for yelling at him only because he was trying to help. We grabbed some doughnuts that Zara's personal assistant bought for her as she was getting ready for the show; knowing Zara she wouldn't eat anything (not even drink water) whenever she is wearing an expensive dress. So, there was eleven out of twelve doughnuts left. Pasher and I looked at each other in glory at the sight of these fresh doughnuts. As I went to grab them, Pasher went to collect a large paper shopping bag so we could store all the food in it. Then I looked for more. Considering how rich my mother was, she had a whole wall full of sweets.

As we had gathered everything by the front door, two bright lights came up from behind the hill; we knew that was the taxi (because we had a really quiet street), so we rolled everything outside next door to the gate. I came back to lock the door, but emotions came flooding back. I ambled inside and took a second to remember all the memories. After a couple of moments I heard my door handle from my bedroom change, I knew the man was awake, it did scare me a little, so I quickly whispered 'Goodbye' and creaked the door shut and locked it.

Miraculously, everything had already been packed into the taxi, but thinking about it I did take my time to say goodbye. As I sat in the back seat, with my new buddy Pasher, I gazed into the boot to check that they hadn't left anything. They didn't. So, we set off.

Ten minutes into the journey, after staring at the beautiful, sparkly lights in the sky, I remembered something. It was Dean; I had completely forgot about him! But, where did he go when I almost drowned in the pool? I reached for my phone and looked for messages, I soon realised that I had my new (yes, new phone already, it was right beside me when I woke up, all started up and everything) phone on silent this whole time. (Zara did not want it to wake me up.) I had reached the number of fifty-two messages from him. They were all worrying messages too, this made me feel awful. I couldn't ask to go back because Pasher said that Zara was on her way home. I just had to change my thoughts. I felt hungry, so I had a doughnut.

"Here are some photos of Zara with her celeb friends. She looks really content. If you look really close into her eyes, she really wants you to be there," Pasher said with happiness.

There was the guilt again, but this time I wasn't going to freak on him. "Yeah. I'm glad she's mostly happy though." Then it went silent for a few seconds. "Hey, um... Pasher, who was that man who saved me?" I asked, having a thought that it was my dad, but then thinking twice about how crazy that is.

"That man was um... your real dad's twin brother," he said with a gentle ease, smiling instantly after to make it seem like a good thing.

I was shocked, did I just hear him correctly? "Wait, why does he show up and not my dad? Also, why now?" I stared at Pasher.

"Well, he also never knew you existed until Zara phoned him up a few days ago, she didn't tell any of her family when she was pregnant. I know you had a dad with Jane, but he isn't related to you at all, that whole family with Jane was fake, well, you know what I mean. Your real dad is a director in Switzerland. He still doesn't know that you exist because your parents split up when Zara found out she was pregnant. So, basically your dad knows that she has a child, but he has never made any effort to find you. Your uncle, the one who saved you, is looking after your mum to offer comfort, but often goes on holidays to go back to his own wife. Zara hadn't seen him for quite a few months, so, he travelled from New Zealand to come and see you before the Show to meet you and send his love, because Zara told him that you were nervous. As he arrived, he described to have heard screaming from Zara and a girl, so he rushed around the side of the house, but the gate was locked so he had to rush through the front door and through the whole downstairs to get to you, that's why you were under the water for a while, if you were wondering," Pasher explained.

"Where were you guys?" I asked, rising back up in my seat.

CHAPTER 20

"Well, I was taking care of Zara's hand, the others were getting the first aid kit and some towels. We knew he was out there with you, otherwise we would have come out much sooner." He hesitated. "I have a question, you don't have to answer it, but..."

"I didn't mean to jump off, I just wanted to sit on the roof for some privacy. Saying it out loud, it does sound really stupid, but in my mind, I just needed to find the quietest place. It wasn't what you thought," I reassured him.

"OK, good. I was really worried. But, if you just jumped into the pool, why didn't you come up?"

"Because the force of the crash injured my neck and the whole adrenaline and anxiety thing made me numb and zoned out. I think I was just so scared; I did not even think of moving. Besides, the dress weighed me down." We both giggled.

"That's what happened. Well then next time I'll know to pick you straight back up in any situation." We both laughed. "OK, I'm going to have a sleep until we get there so, if you need anything just give me a shake." He winked.

"OK." I giggled. I wrapped myself in the blanket and went on Instagram to check out some more photos of their evening. They all looked flawless, but in my opinion, Zara looked the best.

As the morning came to greet us (it was five in the morning and the sun was out and yes, it took us three hours to get to the airport), with the sun climbing the mountain and the dew setting on the grass, I was still awake and not tired because I passed out yesterday at 1pm, well around that time, and I slept until 1:30am so I had many hours of sleep, just shifted backwards, a lot.

On the other side of the seats, Pasher was passed out, still. I do not know how people can just fall asleep in cars, busses, aeroplanes, or even saying that, any moving object. Anyway, my mind was full. It was plastered with regrets, anxiety and stress. But that soon went away when we arrived at the airport and I was distracted.

"Pasher! We're here!" I repeatedly poked him in the shoulder with a gigantic smile sketched across my face.

"What?" he moaned while stretching. "What is it?" He opened his tired eyes. "That was the worst sleep of my life!" He became embarrassed because he remembered that the taxi driver was listening. "Sorry, sir. Great driving, OK got to go." He rushed out of the car.

I stayed seated, grabbing my belongings. "Sorry sir, he's a rough sleeper. But thank you." I stepped outside, stretching my legs. "Pasher there's one thing. I didn't book a flight; I was too preoccupied with thoughts," I rambled, reaching over to get my suitcase, well, three suitcases.

"Good job I did. As you were gazing out of the window, I booked us the private jet," he proudly boasted, lifting my suitcase out of the boot. "It doesn't matter anyway because you're too young to book yet." He lifted the last piece of luggage out the boot.

"Thank you, anyway we ready to go?" I laughed. Pasher shut the boot and hit it twice to give a signal that we were done.

"Of course!"

We ambled to the security and got through quickly. Remember this was my first time going to an airport being "wealthy". As we would normally wait in a room to be called, this time we just walked through a completely empty room and straight onto our own plane.

OMG! This was amazing, it was so luxurious, and we had our own hostess to get food at any time. I sat down and took a picture of my view and posted it on Instagram, captioned 'My view on private jet! So excited.' I waited a few seconds and as it was loading to send, it hit me, I just remembered that Dean was following me, so he would find out that I was leaving. I tapped my phone to prevent it from sending, but it did nothing. It was sent. I mean I could have just turned off my data, but I was too stupid to think of that. (By the way, Zara doesn't know that I have an Instagram account, so I wasn't about to pee myself.) Pasher returned from the toilet and buckled in. My face was in a state of shock. I buckled in slowly and held tightly onto the armrest. (I was a bit nervous to ride on an aeroplane again, since last time it didn't go so well, but in life you just have to get over things to grow, so I was ignoring my thoughts and smiled at Pasher.)

We took off so smoothly down the runway and got in the air in no time. (I would rather take a public flight because I feel safer when there's more people, I don't know why, I guess my mind just thinks like that. Even though I've been on a plane crash with many other people, I would still prefer that than this, you know?)

"Are you alright, Nova? Having second thoughts?" he presumed.

"Actually, no, it's something completely different. I'm going to go to the toilet." I unbuckled and stood up.

"Nova! You can't take the seatbelt off yet, we're not properly in the air!" He held out his hand to stop me from passing. I knew he cared about me, but sometimes I just need to be independent.

"Yeah, but I'm going to pee myself all over these lovely seats that I have to spend my seven hours in. So, I'm going." I pushed his hand out of the way. Then he grabbed my wrist.

"Nova, you're going to risk your life to not dirty a seat. I mean we have ten other seats in here to sit on." He panicked.

"I love you, Pasher." I snatched my hand back and went behind the wall where they would make our food, to think of a plan. In doing so I saw a parachute. I remembered that I did parachuting with my fake dad when I was younger. I knew all the tricks and how to glide and land. This was dangerous, but worth a try. Still I had no actual plan of what on earth I was doing, saying that, I had no clue why I decided to jump, I just needed to get on the ground and phone Dean.

I clipped it onto my body, flung on the glasses, tied my hair back and took a deep breath. I worked out how the lock worked on the door from reading the sign from a distance. I waited a couple seconds and went over it a few times. Then I ran to it in Pasher's sight and speedily followed the instructions, and before I knew it, it was open, all I had to do was push it.

He was looking at his phone, so he didn't realise what I was doing. "Tell Zara I love her if I don't make it!" I shouted to get a reaction. He looked up in a shot and went as pale as can be.

"Nova, what on earth are you doing?! Put the parachute down and let's talk. You don't have to do this. You know very well how this could end. Please come to me and let's talk, I can help I promise." He slowly unbuckled his belt and step by step he walked towards me, holding out his hand.

"I love you, but, I'm sorry." I smiled with a tear.

"Nova, you can tell them that you love them, all we have to do is turn this plane around. Sweetie, listen to me, we can get through this." I looked at the door. "Nova, look at me!"

"Bye." I looked back at him. I kicked it open, getting sucked out by the violent winds created by the turbines.

"NO!!" Pasher screamed.

I was flailing around in circles, I couldn't control the spin, but I did something that helped to slow it down. I spotted where I wanted to land, so I clapped my hands together in front of me and did the same with my legs behind me, so I was like a toothpick, which speeded me up. I glided to where I wanted to go.

In the air, I felt so free, I was like a bird. The wind in my face and the flying creatures swooping with me, it was a moment to remember.

I was getting close to land, closer to my destination. I pulled the ripcord and shooting out was my parachute. I rapidly slowed down and came to land with my feet running. I hadn't done this in a while, so as I landed, I dropped badly on my ankle. I smiled in relief, not really caring about my wounded foot, but caring more that I was alive and that I still had some tricks up my sleeve.

CHAPTER 21

I unclipped the harness and stood up looking at the plane I had jumped out of. To my surprise, it had fully turned around and was coming down fast. I stood in shock, then I ran for my life leaving my parachute behind because they would see it moving from the plane.

On the other side of the field that I sprinted across, I found a large birch tree to hide behind. I crouched down giving myself a front-row seat to the landing. A humongous blast of wind blew right through me, or as it felt. It was like you were in a 4D cinema where you get all the special effects. I squinted into the distance noticing that Pasher was not taking his time getting off the plane.

I steadily scrambled to my feet, bending over, trying not to make any sudden movements to make myself visible. I cut a hole through the hedge with the farmers' pliers that he forgot to bring in, so I could get through to the other side and start my journey to Dean. But obviously everything with me never goes smoothly; my foot got stuck in the hedge with the brambles, they were all digging through my skin and as I yanked my leg out, they tore through my leg leaving bloody cuts.

"Ahhh!" I screamed mercifully in agony. Then I noticed Pasher running towards me dropping everything he was carrying.

"Nova, I'm coming!" he shrieked back. Now, Pasher thought I was in discomfort because I had broken a leg or something from parachuting, but he was drowned in confusion when he got to me. "Thank GOSH you're still alive. Nova, how stupid are you? Do you even know how worried I was? I almost had a heart attack."

Then he noticed my destroyed leg caked in blood. "OMG! There's blood. I can't deal with blood, ew! Can we get a paramedic over here?!" he bellowed back to the plane. The paramedics came rushing out of the plane, well, they weren't doctors, they were air hostesses but, that was all we had.

"I'm sorry. Pasher, I'm sorry. I am so impulsive. Why did I do this?" I cried, squeezing my leg in pain. Pasher leaned over and gave me a hug to cheer me up.

"Hey, you're not silly. I mean you know how to sky dive and not many kids can say they can. I know you're in a bad state of mind right now with everything going on, but things will get better I promise. You just can't keep doing this to me or anyone for that matter, OK?" He squeezed me.

I nodded.

"Hey, I learnt from experience because I was homeless a couple of years ago. I was alone, and I couldn't do anything but believe that something was going to get better. Your mother actually found me and complimented my make-up. That's how it all started; I was extremely lucky." Then the air hostess girls came to fix me up so Pasher sat behind me to hold me up while they worked on my leg.

"Anyway, she needed a new personal make-up artist, but she couldn't find one that she really liked, so she thought that she would let me have a go. She let me stay with her for countless nights. She started paying me to do her make-up and after a few weeks I could afford my own apartment. That was how well she paid me. That was also the time when she told me about you, five years ago. You meant the world to Zara, she would get emotional every time she talked about you, that's why you mean the world to me, because she took care of me and I would do anything in return. She would always say to me, 'If we do find my baby, keep her so safe whenever I'm not around, I would love her too much to lose her again.'" He squeezed me and then rubbed my forehead, calming my nerves down.

"Thank you Pasher, I love you. I will always protect you too." I dozed off to sleep because all this drama was getting too much for my brain to handle.

An hour later (as I was told, yet again, I was told a lot of things because I was unconscious for a lot of it.) I woke up in the plane seat that was laid flat like a bed. I was so cosy. I placed my hand down the side of the seat to turn the bed back into a chair so I could sit up. Pasher was wiped out covered in blankets. I softly moved my duvet to the side and stood up. My legs had been cleaned from all the blood, but I was still dirty, so I tip-toed to the bathroom to have a shower and before I knew it, I heard a voice.

"Nova, what are you doing?" Pasher squinted and stretched. "Oh no, you're not going to jump out again, are you?" He stood up in a shot whipping the duvets to one side.

"No." I laughed. "Just going to the bathroom. I'm having a shower so I'm clean and fresh ready to see my family." I walked out of the room and locked the bathroom door and had a warm, fresh shower. As I came out, I lathered my body in lotion and dried my hair. I wandered out of the bathroom with my robe to collect some clothes to wear.

I scrummaged through my bag and found a lovely denim crop top with a denim skirt. For shoes I had brought matte brown heels, and I also had a denim mini purse to complete the outfit. I went back into the main room to sit and chat with Pasher.

"Hey, Nova. You look lovely," he announced, putting his reading book aside.

"Why thank you," I answered, sitting down. "By the way, thanks for the comforting news you gave me. It has made me look better at this scenario." I smiled, crossing my legs.

"Anything for you. Can I do your hair? I brought extensions!" He excitedly waved them in the air. I nodded. I turned around in my chair and we made a little salon with his tools. Then he stopped talking and became suddenly serious. "Um, Nova I have something to tell you."

I quickly became concerned. "Yeah? Is there something wrong with my hair?"

"No. Something else I didn't tell you. You know that you didn't want anyone to know that you were Zara's daughter yet, because then you would become famous and have paparazzi following you?"

"Well, I didn't mind some people knowing. But, carry on."

"During the Award Show, when Zara was being interviewed, she was asked, 'Would you ever have kids?' Her answer kind of slipped out and she said that she already has one. Then she described you, showed pictures of you, and as she won her award..."

"Wait she won?!" I got excited, forgetting everything.

"Yeah she did. But she told everyone about you. There were millions of people watching the TV last night. I only found out because as we landed to go and get you, all my messages came through as I took it off 'aeroplane mode'. Zara has gone ballistic because she can't find you, I haven't texted her back yet."

"OMG! How bad?"

"305 messages, 36 missed calls and 18 FaceTimes." I instantly thought that we were dead when she found us.

"We are never going back, OK? She'll kill us." Pasher carried on with my hair.

"Yeah, we're never going back."

I was so comfy and relaxed as I was getting my hair done because I was alone with my new friend with no worries. I loved getting my hair done, it is the best feeling in the whole world, well in my opinion.

Before I became famous, I only loved attention more than anything because barely anyone in school or in my fake family would pay attention to me other than Jane, but I'd rather forget her, so I just wanted someone to talk to, but now all I want to be is alone because there are too many people wanting to talk to me. When I was younger, I always wanted more attention than my sister, Jasmine. *JASMINE! OMG!* I thought to myself. I had completely forgotten her. I yelled at Pasher, "Pasher! You need to call Jasmine as soon as we land! It's an emergency, with my sister."

Pasher jumped out of his skin and into the air dropping the comb on the floor. "OK! Who's Jasmine, again?" Looking confused, picking up the comb.

"My sister. My adopted sister. My fake family sister," I stated. "Anyway! I need to see her. It's an emergency." I pulled out my phone.

"Geez. You may be a child, but you are bossy, maybe this life was for you." I kicked him gently. He laughed. "But, anything for you. What would you like me to tell her?" He brought out his notepad to take notes, leaving my hair in a mess.

"Um... say that, I want to meet with her at our auntie's house. Also, book a first-class seat for her on the aeroplane and anything else she wants, and if she wants to bring someone she can. Just a reminder she's in the army, so you're going to have to talk to the boss too, say she's going to stay here for two weeks. Thank you," I rambled.

"Anything else, Madame?" he announced sarcastically.

"Yeah, when we land can you order me a green smoothie with

some mango? I'm feeling healthy." I started to play an offline game.

"OK, but as we get there, we're staying in a hotel for a night and the make-up artist will be there in the morning and I'll do your hair, just in case you thought we were going tonight." He stated reading off his calendar on his phone. I asked a few more questions.

"Will there be paparazzi at the airport?" I anxiously asked, sitting on my hands and biting my lip after turning off my phone.

He took a deep breath. "Maybe but, if Zara doesn't know that you're here, how can they?"

"Well I was thinking of texting Zara as soon as we land," I said.

"Well, in that case, I'll book another bodyguard for you." He smiled. "Right, calm down and enjoy the ride, we have a very busy arrival."

So, I gazed straight out of the small oval window at the clouds and smiled, bracing myself for a new epic journey.

CHAPTER 22

Another hour later, after a smooth ride through the clear sky, we landed nicely on the runway at the Australian airport. I gathered my phone, lip gloss and roll-on perfume and placed them all into my designer bag. Pasher packed everything away whilst I gazed out of the window viewing the surroundings.

As I stared to my right in sight of the people-filled building (airport), to my horrifying surprise, the huge glass window had countless paparazzi behind it all taking photos of our plane. My reaction was to pull down the cover, but I was in shock at how many there were, with the concentration of flashing lights and people waving compared to our plane, it did freak me out. After a while, Pasher saw my facial expression and how still I was just glancing out of the window; he had to come over and shut the cover for me.

As I was now back to myself, I picked up my white faux fur coat and swung my arms into the sleeves and held my denim mini purse with my pinkie. Yes, it was that small.

"How are paparazzi here? I haven't had any signal to tell Zara. I'm so confused." I pulled the sleeves down to cover my hands.

"I'm confused too, there's no way they could have figured out that we were here." Then Pasher had a moment of realisation. "OMG!" He rushed to the pilot's cabin. I followed, intrigued as to what had come to Pasher's mind. "Thank you, sir, for the lovely ride but, you didn't contact Zara at all, did you?" He leaned up against the co-pilot's seat.

"Yes, I did, just before we took off. Is everything alright, sir?" he questioned.

"Yes, everything's fine, do you know where she is now?" I asked, being more paranoid coming into his sight.

"Just before we took off, I sent her an email to say that you were leaving to come here, only because whenever anyone uses her jets, she always wants me to inform her about it directly. Then when we got ready to go. After your surprise skydive, I checked my emails and she got on a plane straight after the event. She seemed very angry and panicky from her writing from the email and she asked me to tell Pasher to keep you very safe." He calmly answered, "From the tracker on this plane's screen it shows their plane and where it is, it roughly states that she's an hour away from us."

Pasher and I glanced at each other in horror. "Thank you so much, sir," I announced, then we both hurriedly walked off the plane with our hand luggage and made for the terminal, with our bodyguards waiting at the doors of the airport. As we were guided by the bodyguards to the sitting area, I was too scared to glance at the huge crowd through the small window, so my bodyguard went to stand in front of the window, which I thought was very generous. When I sat down next to Pasher, I got served my smoothie and mango and Pasher had some tea with oat biscuits. Then Pasher's guard went to talk to mine by the window about where we needed to go, and the safest route possible for me.

I took a sip of my smoothie and licked my lips. "Pasher, I don't even get it. How do paparazzi know where celebrities are all the time?"

"For some, including Zara, their managers inform them, so they get some pictures for the press. That's not the case for all celebrities, but for Zara it is."

"Does she like paparazzi?"

"On her good days, yes. I mean she always talks to them on her good days, but bad days she covers her face."

"Can't she just ask her manager not to tell the photographers where she is on her bad days?"

"No, that's not how it works. You see being a paparazzi, it's a job, you get paid to take photos. So, you can't really take that away from them, because their photos go into news articles and magazines to create mega amounts of money and to make entertainment for their fans. Now, since you're famous because you are the daughter of an international actress that is so loved and praised for her work, all of her fans, or most of them anyway, will be all over you." He did a lot of hand actions all throughout this talk.

"What do you mean by, 'most'?"

"That was not an insult, that just means that some people will love you just as much as her, and some will become jealous that they aren't you and will hate you. I'm not saying they will, it's just an assumption because that what happens a lot within this industry. But, that's why Zara is your mum because she can one, put up with it and two, is so protective of you. I don't fully understand why you don't like this life, tell me again."

"Not everyone born wants to be famous or wants to be in the spotlight 24/7. Yes, I like my once in a while treat or attention, like on my birthday, but not every single day of my life when people can see my every move. Don't get me wrong, I love presents, but the truth is, I don't think Zara understands that all I want is her motherly love, like a hug or a forehead kiss, not an expensive object. Even a hug will make my day. I just need to get away from this, but now that people know who I am, there's no turning back. People will know who I am forever." I sulked just realising that I am now famous, literally over a couple of hours. Some will call this extremely lucky and some will see it as a nightmare.

"Don't worry about it, you have me and everyone else here to support you and make you feel like someone special; I promise. No one is going to put you down on this family's watch."

"Thanks. But, Pasher, here's my next problem for you, I know I shouldn't worry about this but, I don't have a photogenic face so, what do I do when we go through the paparazzi? What face do I make? What do I even say? Should I cover my face with something?" I worried.

"Calm down, baby girl, you're perfect. You are so unique in your own way you don't need to worry about a thing, no one else on this entire planet has the same facial features as you, you need to flaunt them and be proud. But don't say anything to them, just walk by. Although, I thought you would've needed a pair of sunglasses to fight against the flashing lights, so I brought some from your wardrobe. Zara actually bought these a while ago when she did her first shop for you, way before she knew you, and thought that these would come in handy." He reached into his bag and pulled out another pair of designer glasses; this whole "designer" thing will never end. He handed them over and they were huge vintage retro black sunglasses. They were as big as my face. I loved them. It almost felt like a face shield.

"Thanks." I laughed at their size.

"I know they're big, but they are eye-savers. Well, saying that, they're face savers!" He winked. As we chatted for a few minutes, my bodyguard Chris came over and whispered to us that it was time to leave. Yes, I did find it weird that he whispered to us, but everything was now so secretive, he could not even talk to us properly without people knowing what we were saying to put it in the magazine as the front page.

Breaking News:
Nova Whittle gets a message from her bodyguard saying, 'It's time to go, the car's outside.' Next to her is a hairdresser named 'Pasher', who is Zara Whittle's personal hairdresser and he replies with, 'OK, thank you.'

I mean can you imagine that? It would be so boring, but people would do anything for money these days. Anyway, I nodded back and stood up clutching my mini purse with three fingers, I don't think my palms have ever been so sweaty in my life, I just had to think that they were all here for me and would never attack me.

As soon as I stood, instantaneously the crowd started to scream and call out my name. This did make me feel special inside, I can't lie, but my emotions were so tired mixed with anxiety from every little detail that it made me want to leave.

Pasher came right away beside me, held my hand and whispered in my ear, "You can do this, I've got you and you're safe so don't panic. You also look beautiful." I smiled so hard I just couldn't resist giving Pasher a hug. He hugged back so tight.

Then from the crowd I heard an "Aw!" That just made me feel uncomfortable.

"Just ignore them." Pasher knew I felt a certain emotion because he did too.

"Right, let's do this!" I whispered to myself.

The waitress opened the door for me as I walked behind Chris in front and behind me was Pasher and his bodyguard. As soon as I stepped outside, all I heard was screaming, questions and my name being yelled. The worst thing was that we had to walk through them, through the crowd because there were no barriers; I wish they had a different route for us to go through, but it was all used for the public. I tried to smile at the flashing lights, but there were so many people yelling at me to look at them for a picture, I became dizzy and I felt like the world was slowly closing down on me, I soon felt claustrophobic. Suddenly, my heart started pounding much more than before, almost like I had ten coffees at once, my breathing became intense and as I turned around to Pasher I started to find it hard to breathe like my air hole was trapped by mucus, clenching hard onto his arms falling to the floor.

"Pasher, I can't breathe!" Pasher caught me from falling.

"Hey baby, I've got you. Do not worry. Keep breathing." You know, I know he's not a doctor, but when you can't breathe, why do people say back, 'Just keep breathing', like I haven't tried that already?

Luckily, before I knew it Chris was sweeping me up in his arms and carrying me through the crowds like the hero he is. I saw Pasher looking concerned from behind using his purse to help cover his face from pictures, holding my hand that was dangling down Chris's back. As I now felt less nervous because I was being held by a strong person, my hearing was becoming clearer as my ears cracked, then I started to hear each question one by one.

"Nova, are you alright?" I was guessing this was from me falling. "Nova, what is it like having a famous mum?" What can I tell you? I knew this question would appear. "Hey, Nova. Do you have a boyfriend, or will Zara not let you have one?" This was one I did not expect.

As we reached the outside, rushing to the Range Rover waiting for us, we still had crowd of people running after us, it was like the apocalypse that I started.

As Chris opened the car door for me, he gently placed me in the back seat, grabbing a neck pillow from the boot to help keep my head up straight. Pasher speedily jumped in the car after me and he landed sideways and slammed the door shut. (Just to let you know, I still had the huge glasses on.) Whilst Chris sat in the front next to the driver and the other went on a motorcycle behind us. (There were actually a few that jumped into their cars and started to follow us, but this was no surprise, I mean at least they weren't allowed to come into the hotel.) Chris yelled at the driver to go because crowds of people were up against the car windows all around, even on the roads blocking traffic, just to get a picture of me, but we drove off quickly. You could definitely describe it like a car chase, but we were the ones being chased. I'm not going to pretend like this whole chase was an awful memory, it was kind of awesome. I made me feel exhilarated. Like I was in an action movie.

"OMG, babe are you alright?" Pasher placed his hand on my head, it was lovely and cold to soothe my headache. Nobody in this car knew about my breathing issue, so I decided to tell Pasher all about it. I saw Chris listen in, so he knew for next time.

After that, I laid my head against the window, still in the neck cushion to try and get even more rest, knowing so far, I had failed to get any.

Running away from this life is even harder than living it.

A few minutes after the driver had realised that three paparazzi cars were following us, he drove a lot quicker to try and lose them. It never worked. We almost lost them at traffic lights, but they still found us.

CHAPTER 23

As we got to the hotel an hour later, it started to get late again, and there was no private parking behind the hotel, so we had to get out in public to walk in.

The driver parked up and the bodyguard Jake, on the motorcycle, made a path for us to walk through, but I still felt dizzy gazing in the opposite direction to the open door at the crowd starting to gather. Chris got out and walked around to my door and lifted me up like a child, along with my hand luggage and carried me through the mountains of people collecting together (even people walking by stopped and started screaming, they didn't even know who I was, well I was presuming anyway) and into the reception area.

Chris placed me onto the seat next to Pasher, then Jake and Chris went back out to get the rest of the luggage from the boot. Pasher stood up and picked me up off my seat and into his arms with my legs around his stomach; he was a real father figure to me. He rubbed my back and walked around the room making it more relaxing for me. As the guards came back in, they got a luggage trolley and rolled that after us to the elevator. Whilst still in Pasher's arms, I became so sleepy, but still so shocked by the amount of people who congregated so quickly just to see me. At least I had something to dream about.

So, I closed my eyes and tried to go to sleep before I heard Chris whisper to Pasher, "Is she alright?"

"Yeah, just really shocked by what just happened I guess, poor thing, she must be exhausted right now." Pasher swayed his body from left to right repeatedly. The elevator door opened and Pasher walked down the hall with my hands swinging behind him, to go and find our room.

Jake opened the door with the key (which in this case was a card that you swipe) and placed our luggage spread out all over our suite floor. Then they went to their rooms to rest after checking that we were alright.

So, in our room we had two bathrooms, three king-sized beds, two make-up stations, a walk-in wardrobe and a large balcony looking over Sydney. Wow, it was beautiful.

Well, this room was over $20,000 a night and Pasher does get well paid, he's also a millionaire, buts there's no surprise there – anyone who works for my mum will eventually become wealthy, she's too generous. Anyways, Pasher gently placed me in the middle of my heaven bed and went in my suitcase and searched for my PJs. I heard the rustling, so I sat up and stretched, feeling a little lightheaded on the way.

"Nova, you should be sleeping, go back to rest, sweetie." He came over and sat whilst he rubbed my shoulders. "Are you OK now?" He smiled.

"Yeah, I think I'm better. I do still feel a little uneasy but, better. I just need to go to the toilet and change for bed. Then can we chat after?" I yawned.

"Yeah, of course. Be careful though, I'll be in here if you need anything." He helped me up off the bed and into the bathroom.

I splashed some cold, crisp water on my face even though I washed it two hours ago in the plane shower, I added some creams and lip balm and then I went to the toilet. I came out all fresh but a little peckish, but this is normal. I steadily wobbled out clinging onto the wall and walked to my luggage bag and pulled out my silk PJs and silk cushion cover for my pillow.

Pasher was on the bed with a cold rag on his forehead to calm him down from the ridiculous day we had just been through.

"You holding up alright over there?" I said, a little concerned, splashed with some laughter.

He sat up quickly. "Oh yeah, just a little headache. But, how are you, still dizzy?"

"I'm perfect now, no headache or dizziness. I think the cold water did it."

"Yeah you are, that's my girl." He laughed, standing up, coming over to hug me. It was a very reassuring hug, it's what I needed. "Also, the maid came in whilst you were in the bathroom, and she hung up all of your clothes."

"That's cool. I will thank her later."

I started to put on my PJs, and we had a knock on the door. It was a very vicious knock.

CHAPTER 24

I rushed dressing whilst Pasher went to the door very slowly giving me time to finish. I slipped on my silk slippers and combed my hair. Pasher peeped through the peephole and he saw Chris. We were both confused because we thought he was worried about something, so I ran up next to Pasher and we sluggishly opened the door in caution.

"Sorry to bother you ladies, but someone is here to see you," he worriedly said. I looked at Pasher and grabbed his hand as we both steadily walked down the corridor after Chris.

Then Jake opened the door and I walked around the corner to the beds and... "MUM!?" I swear my heart skipped a beat, then my jaw dropped.

"NOVA!" She ran up to me and hugged me so tight I could've popped. "I thought I lost you, my baby girl. NEVER do that to me again! Do you hear me? I'm serious!" She finally let go and kissed my face all over. Then she pulled me over to her side, yanking my hand from Pasher's. Then she looked at Pasher with a bare face. Then followed with the death stare.

"You IDIOT! I trusted you. I've already lost her once; do you want me to suffer again?" Zara's voice cracked into a cry. Pasher started to tear up.

"I'm so sorry, Zara, I'm sorry." He looked so weak. "I'm sorry," he softly said.

"MUM! I made—" I tried interrupting her. But she ignored me.

"WHAT ARE YOU SORRY FOR, PASHER? TAKING MY DAUGHTER AWAY FROM ME?!" She was extremely angry, she almost hit Pasher, I didn't know she was this scared for my life.

"MUM! I MADE PASHER DO THIS!" I broke into rage. I couldn't stand Pasher being treated this way after everything he had done for me. Zara turned to me with big eyes full of tears.

"What?" She strained her voice, quickly gazing back at Pasher who was in pieces. Pasher then fell to the floor in grief, with tears flooding his face.

I ran over to him, but Zara pulled me back. "Stop! You have said enough, Mum. I did this, not him. Not anybody else, it was all me. I wanted to leave; I hated this whole thing. I don't even know you, even if you are my mum, I don't want to stay with you, I want to go back home, this is all way too much for me. I love you, but I can't." She let go and fell to the ground. I hugged Pasher so tight and wiped his tears away. "I'm sorry, so, so sorry."

I helped Pasher up and we ran back to the room both crying. Pasher was in front so as he ran in the room first, Zara followed us down the corridor and managed to grab my hand from behind and dragged me back a few steps. "Baby you can't leave me, I'm your mother and I love you endlessly, please, I have tried to find you for so long, I would die if you weren't still here. I promise I can make it work, I promise, please let me try, baby." She sat on the floor literally begging. She couldn't even stand. I didn't know what to do. I was just a child.

"Mum, I love you too. This is so hard for me, because I want to be with you every day, but I hate the way your life runs. We'll never be together; you'll be too busy all the time and I'll just be used for help. It's unfair for me, Mum, it's not fair for me." I wiped my tears away. Zara stood up and began kissing my forehead with her weary lips. "You can't treat Pasher like that, he's the most loyal and respectful person I've ever met, he doesn't deserve it. Especially from you." I pushed Mum's hands away and ran into the bedroom locking the door behind. Zara ran towards me and repetitively pounded on the door, begging for forgiveness, just to let her in.

"Please baby, let me in! LET ME IN!" she cried. It was so hard to listen to while I was cuddled up by Pasher's side on the bed waiting for it to stop. Just waiting. Soon Chris came and carried her back to their room to calm the noise in the hallway. All we could her was screaming to let her go and to open the door.

I slept with Pasher because I was so scared. The screaming was played like a broken record in my brain, over and over it was breaking my heart. Pasher was rubbing my head, humming all night until I fell asleep. I did in the end.

CHAPTER 25

Around 9:30am, room service knocked on our door with fruit and waffles. I had ordered some water and orange juice which we ate on the balcony overlooking a lovely park a distance away.

"How are you today? Are you ready to see your family?" He smiled with a strawberry in his mouth.

"Very excited! Just nervous to see Mum, I guess." I gulped down my water.

"Everything will be OK; I'll be there right by your side. Also, to cheer you up the make-up artist will be here in an hour." He held my hand across the table.

"OK, I'll have a shower and pack, but can you tell the make-up person to go light?"

"Just for you, yes. Also, you do not need to pack, the staff do it here for you." He drank his water and grinned.

So, I hopped off and took a refreshing shower, again. I brushed my teeth and hair and lathered on lotions. As I walked out in my robe I put on some underwear and sat in the new "throne" and Pasher started to do my hair and soon after the make-up artist came in and started on the art piece, me.

I had a huge bow in my hair with loose strands hanging down, with a very natural make-up look, nothing too much. For my outfit, I had light brown dungarees with a white long-sleeve shirt, with black heeled boots and the extravagant sunglasses. I also had a clear purse that just had my phone in.

"Let's take on the world, Pasher, let's take it on by storm!" We walked out into the hallway, hopped in the elevator to take us to the lobby to meet up with Chris and Jake to get into the pink limo. Amazingly, as we strolled outside, I posed for the paparazzi and happily walked into the limo, but after I sat down a twist in my day was made. A twist I did not want to happen.

CHAPTER 26

I froze in horror. Mouth wide open, vision gone blurry then normal. I blinked and just sat there for a second, still with the door wide open so paparazzi could see in.

I just couldn't do it. "I'm sorry, no, I can't be in the same room as your right now, I couldn't sleep last night, I lived my worst nightmare last night because of you and now you think it's OK for you to even look at me. Chris, I'm going back inside." I saw Zara try and reach for my hand. "Don't, you dare. I wanted to do this by myself, something by myself before you took over my life, I'm seeing my family without you, you can come later, but you WILL NOT take my happiness away today!" I yelled.

I looked around the car to see everyone staring in shock at what they had just witnessed from me. Always the ones you don't expect, they probably thought. They all looked away quickly. Then with the people outside, I just slammed the door shut and sat with my back to Zara and everyone else. Zara did not want to leave.

"Why aren't you leaving?" She didn't answer. "ZARA!" I screamed. "What is wrong with you? You don't have an invitation to stay, so LEAVE!"

I crossed my legs like an angry businesswoman. "We'll try this then." Zara looked happy I was talking to her. "We'll drop you off at the Australian jail so you can see Jane. Remember my fake, abusive, threatening MOTHER, who you gave me too?" Zara's face dropped in fear. "Whilst everyone else in this car goes to see the best side of my fake family, who I call real BECAUSE THEY TREAT ME LIKE FAMILY AND DON'T THROW ME IN THE DEEP END AS SOON AS I MEET THEM!" I again raised my voice at Zara; her face dropped even lower.

She sat back in her seat and started crying. I just sat there feeling helpless. (I didn't want to make her cry, I just wanted her to know that she doesn't understand my problem.)

"Don't cry," I quietly said under my breath.

Zara looked up, with tears filling her face and she still managed to smile, oh her beautiful smile just covered her sadness within a second.

Not going to lie, it did make me feel better, less guilty. My body just took control and I slid across the long seat and wrapped myself around her and gave Zara the biggest squeeze. "I'm sorry. Please forgive me. I shouldn't have shouted or locked you out yesterday. It was really hard for me. But we need to talk after seeing the family." I let go from the hug. She smiled even harder.

"I love you, baby. Of course, whatever you need from now on. I'll be a proper mother; I won't make you do anything you don't want to; I won't overload you with gifts anymore." Then she looked over at Pasher. "And as for you. I'm so sorry, Pasher. I shouldn't have rushed to conclusions. I love you so much and will repay you in any way I can." She smiled.

"There's no need, Zara. You gave me this extraordinary life that I still need to repay you for. So, I know you didn't mean those things, it was just in the heat of the moment. I understand."

"You're the best, Pash." She leaned over and they both hugged it out.

A couple minutes down the road, we stopped.

"Nova, we thought we would stop before arriving at your family's house, if you don't want to go in it's fine," Chris announced. I gazed out of the window and to my surprise, it was the jail. I grabbed my bag and before I left, I asked for just Zara to come, like a mother-daughter duo adventure. But, a very depressing adventure. I had to face her.

We stepped out with no paparazzi in sight, it felt good. I held Zara's hand and we were escorted by the police with our bodyguards behind.

Chris announced quickly, "Nova, just a word of warning, she doesn't know that you've met Zara yet." I looked over at Mum and she gave a reassuring glance and winked.

"We'll give her a nice surprise." Zara smiled.

We went to the interview room and sat in there and waited. It was myself, Zara, Chris and Jake along with two more police officers. "It's going to be OK. Remember I'm your mother, not this nasty woman," I heard in my ear.

"Yeah, but she raised me for ten-plus years, so it wasn't all bad for me," I replied.

"Yeah OK, but I have you now and you're safe. Also, what she did to you in the last couple of weeks, is how much people do bad in their entire life."

"Well, she's out of my life entirely now, this is just going to be a goodbye forever. Nothing more." Zara nodded.

The door unlocked and in came Jane with her all-in-one and cut hair with bruises scattered on her face and arms. But what was a surprise was that she had a big cheesy grin on her face like she wanted to attack me again. At first, she didn't even see Zara, she was so excited to see me as she jumped on the chair excitedly with no chains attached.

"Where did all of the bruises come from?" I asked. If I was to ever rewind in time, I wouldn't have asked this, because she still knew I cared for her, which was her strength and my weakness.

"You know, I'm not a fighter, but every day I will fight to get out of here to come see you, but I'm apparently too dangerous to be let out and they have to get three policemen to lock me back up." She knew she was too dangerous, and she liked it. I was too frightened to roll my eyes in case she jumped across the table, so I cautiously looked around the room at my two bodyguards and two policemen. I felt more protected with an extra person but still really vulnerable that she was two feet across the table.

"Anyway, enough about me, how are you? How do you feel? It has been ages!" She laughed wickedly.

"Is this some kind of joke? You almost killed me that day. You attacked me until I was so weak that I needed a group of people to protect me!" I yelled with hand actions. "You're in here for a long time, for all the bad reasons and I'm so happy about it. Don't make this into something funny, because I've lost you. I've lost someone I've loved BECAUSE THEY COULDN'T CONTROL THEMSELVES!" I screamed at the top of my lungs. I did feel better after that.

"I'm sorry!" she screamed back, but it wasn't meant for an apology, it was meant to intimidate me. "I don't know what happened. I was so happy with you." She calmed down and tried to reach for my face to smooth it, then all the bodyguards came forward and placed their hands in the way. "I was ready to experience life with you, experience happiness." She started to cry, but I thought it was fake. "But I lost it. Because I'm stupid. BECAUSE I'M STUPID!" She shot up from her chair and slammed her fists down on the table. Zara and I jumped; I could feel Zara grab my hand. The policemen took both of her arms and pulled her back.

All of a sudden, Jane looked at Zara and froze. Jane's face became the face of someone who had been betrayed.

Zara pulled me close, holding my arm like a koala bear.

"YOU!" Jane yelled. Realising who she was, she shook her arms out of the policemen's reach. "How did you find Nova? You weren't supposed to, she's mine!"

Then Jane went deep and thought she would make it personal to take control of the conversation. "You have missed over ten years of her life, what a sad and lonely woman you are! You were the one that got rid of her, and left her on my doorstep in the hope that I would take her in." What? I was shocked.

"I didn't do that!" Zara shrieked back.

"That was exactly how it went! We had the greatest bond, and I would have kept her away from you forever because she would have never deserved a person like you. But now you think you can just take her away from me!?" She started to yell and cry at the same time, banging her fists on the wall behind; even in the movies I had never seen an angrier person than her.

"You're sick! You know that?" Zara yelled back. "You're right, I am taking her back, she was always mine, you just couldn't face the truth of not being able to give birth, so jealousy has taken over. She's living with me and you will never see her again after this. It's your last chance to say what you want." I felt sick. I just wanted to get out.

"I never mistreated her before this holiday, we were inseparable! She will never love you more than me for as long as you live." She blew up in fury. I could feel Zara get infuriated.

"She already does love me more than you, you psycho," she replied quieter.

"And what would you like me to say, Zara? What would you like me to do to make you happy?" Jane sarcastically said, tilting her head to the side.

"Right, she has nothing to say to you. I think we should go, Nova." Zara turned to face the door and pulled me with her. I felt agitated that I would never see her again even though she was awful to me, there was a battle of emotions in my head. I still had some compassion for her, for everything she had done for me before. Jane walked fast towards us, scraping the metal chair on the concrete floor as she brushed past it. Everyone took action to block her from us.

"Wait," she desperately said.

"Oh goodie, she has something to say," Zara said as we turned around.

"Mum, please. Let her speak." I walked over to the table and sat on the chair, under the bright light whilst Zara stood behind me with her arms crossed.

"I'm so sorry, I have messed up your life and everyone else's. I would take it back right this second if I could." She reached across the table to hold my hand, but I swiped it away before she could reach, then she gazed at Zara with smirk eyes.

"DON'T YOU DARE!" Zara yelled in panic.

Before I knew it, Jane had leapt over the table and wrapped her arms around me, clinging onto me tightly like I was her prey, which I was. My chair had fallen back, and the room had turned into a war zone. I was pushing my knee into her stomach to get her off. The policemen grabbed her waist and started to pull, Chris was pulling me, it was a true game of tug-of-war, like déjà-vu. Zara started to beat Jane's back with her fists. I was getting exhausted again, being chucked around like a toy.

"Baby, don't leave me here!" was all I could hear from Jane.

Pleading just like last night with Zara.

"Don't listen to her, Nova!" Zara replied.

Now I felt like I had hit rock bottom. My fake mum that had raised me for over ten years was fighting for me to save her and take her back, my real mum was fighting for me to leave Jane and to love her, and all I had wanted to do since I got here was see my true family. My life was liveable before, why did I want to go on holiday this year? I mean there are pros and cons to this situation, I guess it isn't all bad.

As we were separated, Zara walked over to Jane being held by the police and slapped her hard, which created a red rash on the side of her face.

"You ever attack or breathe around my daughter again, I'll kill you." Zara's eyes could kill; one glance and oh my, you are gone.

"Funny, that. You couldn't even defend your own daughter, the guards did all the work. You gave me a back massage more than a beating, so thanks for that, do it again soon?" Jane smiled cruelly, with blood coming from a cut that appeared on her cheek. She really looked drained.

"That's enough! The joke's on you, you're the one in this mess. You're the one who's locked up in a cell! You just can't control yourself, can you?" The policemen dragged her away. Jane did fight them as she kicked and pulled and begged to give me one last kiss.

"Please! Don't take her away from me," she cried; it was surreal.

But then she was gone. Again, taken away from me. "Are you alright? Are you hurt?" Mum patronised me.

"No. Just adrenaline. Can we go?" I just wanted to get out of the room, it got stuffy and had depraved vibes.

Zara hugged me as we walked outside, and the paparazzi managed to capture us coming out as they peeped over the stone wall. Not soon after, questions flew through the air again.

"Why have you come here?"

"What relative is in here?"

I felt intruded.

As we climbed back into the limo, the driver had poured some drinks for everyone to change the dramatic vibe that lingered around Zara and myself (the bodyguards were back to normal because they deal with this every day). I had pink lemonade and cuddled up next to the window away from everyone else at the other end talking about the plans for the rest of day. The driver hadn't started to drive yet as he was getting the sat-nav ready.

Soon Pasher scooted over the long seat and sat next to me; I could see that he just wanted me to forget about it.

"Hey, look, it's over and done with. You never have to see her again, she's out of your life now," he tried to reassure.

"I know, but she really did love me. We were the best of friends; I mean she would have done anything for me. If she wouldn't have taken those drugs, we would be hanging out right now with snacks and drinks in our back garden."

"If she loved you like Zara, she would have never taken those drugs knowing that she could harm you."

"Stop comparing her to Zara! She was the one who taught me how to walk and talk, she was the one who stood by me in my best and worst moments. She was truly the kindest person you would ever meet, but her depression just took control and if she told me about it, I could have helped. But she didn't want me getting gloomy because of her own problems. She was too kind."

"Well, even if she did, she still ended up harming you. You can't love her after what she did, period. Zara would do anything for you and even if she was depressed, she wouldn't take any drugs because she knew that she had a daughter to protect."

"Pasher, stop!" Everyone in the car stopped and stared. "She was in a really dark place and needed someone. She didn't know who to ask for help, she had no guidance, she felt alone. Please stop attacking her because she made a mistake. Even though she attacked me again today—"

"WHAT?!" Pasher exclaimed.

"She just wanted me to stay, she was fully drained out from the abuse she was getting. I could see the harm and misery in her eyes, her soul was dying. I just wanted a moment of where she would listen to me, a moment where I could tell her that I missed her, I missed our hugs, girl trips and funny conversations that would last all night, but she was to desperate to get out, she couldn't think properly. She was scared, I could see it, but she didn't want to show that she was powerless!" I cried, badly.

"Nova, listen. You just can't have any love left for her; she just looks at you like you're her bait. You're not seeing the big picture."

"You're joking, right? You're just messing with me."

"What? No, Nova I'm being serious."

At that moment, I opened the door in full rage, stormed across the pavement and threw my lemonade onto the curb and watched it smash into thousands of pieces. I paced around the corner out of sight.

I couldn't calm down, it's the most infuriating thing when no one understands you, or even tries to listen. I felt like I could have punched a hole through a metal wall.

Soon after, Pasher came running around the corner with everyone else.

"Nova!" he yelled. "What's wrong?"

"You! You are my problem. You're not listening to me. I'm telling you what's wrong, and you're not taking my side of the story. All that you can do for me right now, is leave me alone!" I shrieked at him. He looked frightened.

I fell onto my knees in fury and cried so hard that I thought I was screaming.

Pasher came over and rubbed my back, but I hit him in the arm to get him away.

"Don't touch me! I have had a really rough couple of days, well, weeks. I really thought that you were a friend. But I guess not."

"Nova, I'm so sorry. You're right, I have misjudged everything. I know she made a mistake; I didn't know that she was a loving mother before. In fact, we all thought that she had abused you your whole life. I'm so sorry, I was insensitive."

"You should be the one crying! Not me."

"I know. I promise to be a better person for you."

"Shut up! You're just making things worse. No-one cares about me; NO-ONE CARES ABOUT ME! I'm in so much pain, Pasher. No-one understands. I have lost my best friend, my real mother's too busy for me, I have never met my dad, and I'm lost. I feel so vulnerable to this world, I feel so alone."

"You have all of it wrong. We all love you," he said soothingly. "Zara loves you so much, she would do anything for you. You haven't lost Jane, she's lost you. One day you'll meet your dad, I promise. Don't you forget that I'll always be here for you, no matter how many arguments we have, no matter how many times you yell at me, I'll always be right here by your side. I love you, Nova."

I looked up at him and I felt that all of my emotions had just let go. I felt so dizzy from all the crying, that I just fell asleep in his arms. Dreaming in the clouds, finally calming down.

I remember waking up as Pasher was carrying me back to the car, and whispering, "I love you too." The last thing I saw was Pasher smile.

We then drove to our final destination, when all of a sudden, I woke up out of dead sleep and startled everyone by yelling.

CHAPTER 27

"Dean!" I screamed randomly. "Dean! I need to see him immediately!" Scrolling like a flash through my contacts.

"HEY! Calm down," Zara yelled back. "You can see him when we go back. I promise." She slid over the seats to sit next to me and Pasher.

"MUM! Have you not listened to me, at all? I'm not going back. I've told you!" I turned up the volume. She looked puzzled and shook her head.

"You're not coming back?" she gently said. "I mean where are you going to stay?" The conversation took a pause. I looked at her, emphasising that I was staying with Rachel. "NO, NO, NO! You are NOT staying with them! It is a dump there, baby. I can't have you staying with them, or even LIVE with them. You deserve so much better." She became very impolite towards them, even after all they have protected me from.

"MUM! Stop being so rude, their house is amazing. In my opinion, much better than yours." She frowned her eyebrows. "It's on the beach and is cosy and warm with the fireplace on because it's small and private (emphasis on PRIVATE). It's close to a school and I have cousins there to go on adventures with to help distract me from the world that you have created for me. It's perfect for me. The lifestyle I have always dreamed of." The whole car became quiet.

"Mum...?" There was no sound after that for a while.

Then under her breath she said, "I'm not losing you again..." She gazed out of the window with her head rested against it. After a long hesitation, it started to hail like glass falling on metal, it was so painful to hear that every time my eyelids would glitch. I wanted to get our problem sorted out, so I tried talking again.

"But—"

"I'm not losing you again," she interrupted. Then the rest of the journey to the cousins' house was silent.

CHAPTER 28

As we arrived, the hail had stopped, and the sun appeared. I rushed to be the first to open the door and take a step outside. As the sun sprayed on my face, I applied some lip balm and walked to the front door. Everybody followed behind. The sound of the sea and the warm calming wind felt so naturally pure. I felt at home here. I secretly smiled as I rang the doorbell.

A rare moment passed, then Michael answered the door and I flung my arms around him and swept him off the floor.

"You're back! I've missed you," he happily shouted. I walked in and Michael dragged me to the back garden where everyone was sitting, sunbathing.

"Hey!" I shouted in excitement.

Everyone turned around in a shot with their jaw dropped and ran as fast as they could screaming with joy. Even Aunt May fell off her plastic chair as she moved so quickly. I fell to the ground as they all piled on top. I laughed so hard. I couldn't tell you how happy I was.

Then Zara, Pasher and the bodyguards came out through the back door one by one. As I scrambled to my feet, shaking all the sand off my clothes, I introduced everyone.

Even John was back from the hospital and I gave him a special separate hug because he was still in the recovery process, and I whispered in his ear, "I'm still so sorry. But you look great, I'm so proud."

Then he muttered back, "It isn't your fault remember, and you look gorgeous."

Then out of nowhere, came Uncle Joey from the bathroom. His head did have a huge dent in it, but he looked so strong. "NOVA?!" He ran so fast.

He couldn't stop soon enough so he knocked me over. I laughed so hard that my throat hurt. We rolled over in the sand and hugged each other so tight. Then Michael and Julia joined in. I noticed Zara grabbed Rachel to have a chat inside. But, since we were catching up, I told them about my other life across the seas and how I met Zara. It did sound unrealistic, but they told me they saw the news and thought that they had lost Rachel too. But, the news about my other life mesmerised them.

I wanted to be with my (Fake) family, but I also wanted to know what my mother was talking about inside, so I asked Pasher to go and listen secretly. He was like my personal spy.

I thought it would be the best time to give my presents that I stole from my wardrobe to my cousins as Zara was inside. So, I asked Chris to go and collect the suitcase.

A few hours had passed, and they loved their clothes, but I said to hide them from Zara. Then as it began to get dark and chillier, we went inside to the lounge. Aunt May put on the fire and we changed into our PJs and relaxed under blankets. The bodyguards and Zara borrowed PJs, but Pasher borrowed the PJs from the hotel to wear that he folded in his bag. We then all played board games and watched Rom-Com movies whilst Julia was obsessed with Zara because she was famous.

As it got late, May and Joey brought out cushions and duvets, so we all slept in the lounge with the dying fire and the golden fairy lights around the windows. I've got to say, it was quite magical.

In the morning, early in the morning around six thirty, Zara woke me up quietly and took me on a walk along the beach as the sun was rising. "How did you sleep?" she asked.

"Great, I was warm and comfy and had an amazing dream about how my life wasn't crazy. I dreamt about being with my family, just like last night." I smiled, looking at the smooth sugary sand.

"Good. I want to talk to you about something." She stopped and sat on the grass bank facing the sea. I sat next to her and she wrapped her scarf around us both, it was more like a blanket than a scarf. "What do you want to be when you're older?" She placed her head on my shoulder snuggling in.

"I would love to be a singer. But I have no confidence whatsoever, so I don't know."

"Can I hear you? Just a snippet of a song?" She raised her head and looked at me. "Please?"

I hesitated, but thought, *Why not?* I closed my eyes and sang my heart out, knowing she wouldn't laugh at me if I sounded awful. Anyway, the beach was empty at this time so there was no one else here to judge me.

"OMG. Why haven't you sang for me before? You're amazing! You know I can help you become the greatest singer in the world, I have that power in the industry. Obviously, you are going to have to work for it, but I can help!" She smiled and hugged my body side on.

I smiled back. "Maybe." Thinking about the lifestyle that I would have to have.

"Oh, baby please come home. I love you so much, and all I want to do is keep you safe. I know you love it here; I do too. I was wrong about their house and lifestyle, it's peaceful and personal. But I can give you anything you want, opportunities, clothes, money, cars, education. Mostly, love and happiness." She begged.

"I don't want what you can give me. I just want you to understand that I hate your lifestyle, I love you and your loyalty, but everything else is chaos in my eyes. I can't learn there, be myself there, be natural. The lifestyle you are providing me with is unhealthy, toxic and will make me dependant on you and everything else, for my age anyway. That's not me. The only reason I would be there is for Dean. In fact, I think he's flying over here as we speak. I don't actually know why I got so scared in the car, because I know he's coming here to stay with me. Now there's nothing I would live with you for." I stood up. So did Zara.

"But I can take that all away if..." she pleaded.

"Wait. Last night I told Pasher to spy on your conversation with Rachel."

"What?"

"He said he couldn't believe how much you wanted me to go home with you. He got emotional just listening to you begging to Rachel. Rachel was apparently shocked knowing that I wanted to stay with her, but you just kept begging for me to be with you, and to find a way Rachel could persuade me to stay with you."

"Yeah that happened." She sat on the floor. I gracefully placed myself on the ground next to her.

"I love you, Mum. I've thought about this long and hard; I didn't have a good night last night sleeping, because I couldn't sleep thinking about my decision."

"Please..."

"Wait."

"No, baby please. I love you so much I... I can't..."

"I'm staying with you, Mum. I'm not leaving you," I said. "I'm going home with you."

"What? Really? Oh my gosh! Really?" She leapt from her seating position and landed on top of me, clutching me so tight. "AHHHHHHHH! I'M SO HAPPY!" She kissed my face all over and we rolled all over the sand laughing, smiling, screaming and crying.

I got up and helped her up off the floor. We laughed so hard. "I have a surprise for you," Zara said.

"Mum, don't put me off." After all I had said about not wanting things, she got me another thing.

"No, trust me. You'll love it." She rubbed my arms. Then she brought out her whistle from her pocket and said, "I thought I would have had to use these people to help persuade you." I got confused, did she say 'people'? She covered my eyes and blew the whistle. A few seconds later, she counted down, "3, 2, 1, OPEN!" I kept them close because I was scared.

"Baby come on, open them." I did.

"WHAT! AHHHHHH!" Jaimie and Jasmine were standing right in front of me. "Dad? Sis?" I ran forward to hug them. "I've missed you guys so much. So much has happened, I need to tell you about everything. I never thought I would see you again."

"Hey, we know everything, Zara told us everything. You are the bravest person I've ever met. Jumping out of the plane, two comas, panic attacks and swimming in the middle of the ocean, an attack from Jane, a runaway and landing on rocks. The list goes on. You are a force to be reckoned with. I've, we've missed you so much," Jasmine replied. I've missed her voice and her reassurance so much.

"Yeah. You are a superhero. Your prize was to find out that your mother is rich and famous, and you can have anything you want. What don't you want about that?" Jaimie added.

"I guess you really do know everything." I sat down and everyone else followed and we ended up in a circle. "I have decided to stay with Mum. But, the reason why I don't want to stay is the pressure of how you look every day, and the amount of money Mum spends on me when all of that money can go to charity, which then makes me feel selfish when all I've done is accept it. I guess I'm not ready, to be swarmed by so many people at once. To be treated like the Queen and never being able to understand the true value of money. But I've got to put that all behind me and just go with it."

"I mean, it is a lot. But you can do so much for charity when you are famous because everyone will see you as a role model, so if you set up fundraisers people will donate. Most people will know you and will want to be as good as you, so this is a great advantage," proved Jaimie.

"Yeah you're right. OK then, now that we have that sorted, how long will you be staying for?"

"Well, we'll be going tomorrow morning. I have to get back to my baby and Dad has more customers, for his photography, so we both are very busy," Jasmine tiredly said.

"I'm sorry, did you say you have to get back to your baby?" I was so confused, last time I saw her she didn't even have a boyfriend, which just to say, was two years ago.

"Yeah, I had her five months ago and I'm getting married in two months to my boyfriend Liam. My baby girl's name is Saturn. Liam picked it up from his scientist training, he loves the other planets."

"I'm an auntie?!" I jumped up in excitement, spinning around through the cold morning air.

"Yeah, also you're both invited to our wedding in Wales." I spun even faster. I was super excited. Then we all had a family hug and walked back to get some breakfast with the others.

At 5pm, the doorbell rang. As I was already up coming back from the toilet, I shouted I would get it. I opened the door and on the mat was a note. I looked around to see if anyone was hiding or running, but no one was lurking around.

On the front it said, "*Nova Only*".

It was folded over, so I closed the door and sat on the bench outside. I opened it and it said this.

To my love,

I have missed you so much. A person named Pasher sent me a private jet to get here and see you, because he said you missed me, and you made a mistake. Get dressed in nice clothes and meet me at the end of the beach (just you) in ten minutes.

I love you,

Dean.

Xxx

So, I followed the instructions and put on a white fairy-tale dress, with my hair in beach waves with flowers weaved into it and no shoes because it was the beach.

In my woven bag I had lip gloss, perfume and my phone. I sneaked out and ducked under the window and made a run for it. Two minutes later Dean was in sight, I could see a mat and a basket. When I was ten feet away, I stopped and stared at him, he stared at me. He was wearing a white button-up shirt and blue jeans, with his hair neatly combed.

"You look beautiful, Nova." He smiled. I ran forward with my dress flowing behind and hugged him so tight.

"I've missed you so much. It's been really hard." He rubbed my back.

As we let go, he showed me the basket and mat that he had brought for a picnic, so we sat on the ground together and took a picture to remember this moment. He kissed my cheek and I told him everything that had happened and, that I was staying with Zara partly so I can be with him. Dean loved the idea. He'd brought glazed doughnuts and strawberries with elderflower pressé to wash down the sugar. We watched the sun set below the sea line, and boats docking for the evening. It was very romantic but special because I felt that nothing was wrong, it seemed that all of my worries had gone within one night.

CHAPTER 29

As dusk set upon us early in the morning, I opened my crisp eyelids and panicked because we had slept on the beach for the whole night.

I sat up with my hair in knots and sand in my ear, vigorously shaking Dean to wake up. I noticed that as I did wake up, Dean's arm was wrapped around me. I hated that I had to push it off, it made me feel loved for once.

"What?" he tiredly whined. "What's the rush?"

"We SLEPT on the beach! My mother is going to be so worried! Get up! We NEED to go!" I pulled his arm and helped him stand up.

"OK. Calm down, she'll understand where we were." He tried to reassure me.

"No, she won't, you don't know my mother, she'll think we did something... bad." I hesitated. He just stood there.

"Anyway, last night was amazing. The food and our chats. We have to do this again sometime," Dean said, as we started walking back.

"Yeah, if my mother doesn't kill me. But it was lovely. Where did you get the doughnuts from?" I laughed.

"I actually can't remember." We sniggered.

It was a nice walk along the shore with the orange sun and seagulls calling in the crisp morning air. But, as we got closer to the house,

Zara was sitting outside with a book and a large hat on, like one of those evil stepmothers in films, under the sun umbrella, looking calm although it was just an act. I didn't believe it; even though she was an actress, she couldn't fool me.

"Mum?" I cautiously said.

"Hi darlings. How was your night? It was the perfect weather to sleep on the beach, don't you think?" She stood up. throwing her book in the sand, then finally turning bright red.

"Mum..." I tried to say.

"No, I don't want to hear your excuses, you see this is how it works when you're under my responsibility, Nova." Then she glared at Dean and started to point fingers. "If you want to take my daughter out, you ask me, understand, Dean? I want to know where my daughter is at all times, especially if I've already made the mistake of missing out many years of her life. I'm not going to let you ruin it!" she yelled.

"That's enough, Mum!" I took over. "We're going inside to pack, come in when you have thought about this situation properly and you've calmed down. You know I wouldn't go anyplace stupid; I would ask you if I ever thought about it. He only took me a few yards to the left, not to France." I dragged Dean behind me and started to walk.

"Look! You sleeping on the beach, outside of the walls of the house is still dangerous. What part of that sounds safe? I know some do it in movies, but that's in movies! It's all planned to be safe, reality isn't. Something awful could have happened, and you know that."

"I didn't plan to sleep on the beach, Zara, if that's what you think. I wouldn't scare you like that. We just lost track of time and fell asleep to the sunset, we made a mistake, I get it, but we learn better from our own mistakes. That's a lesson taught."

"Well, don't make that mistake again!" Dean and I left the area and went inside for breakfast.

I saw Zara sit on the bench looking stressed and uncomfortable about the situation; she didn't come in for a while.

After some time, I looked through the window and saw her shedding tears like horse hairs. I ran outside immediately to comfort her.

"Was it me?" I rushed up to her and squeezed her with my arms.

"I shouldn't shout at you like that, I'm sorry," she sobbed.

"Mum, forget about it. You were just being a protective mother. I understand." I tried to comfort.

"Then why did you argue?"

"I was just in the heat of the moment, and I wanted to stand up for Dean, you were a bit aggressive towards him when he was just trying to be nice."

"Pasher said where you had gone, so I didn't want to ruin your date by collecting you like you were still in nursery, so I just went to bed knowing that you would come in yourself. I was just so scared when I woke up and you weren't next to me. I had a panic attack and had to take medication from Rachel." She paused. "I thought that you did a runaway again and you were going to get seriously injured. I couldn't live with myself if that happened when I was the one watching over you."

"Mum, just forget about everything that just happened, OK? I'm fine, I love you and we're just going to carry on."

Then we strode inside and wiped her tears away before anyone got suspicious. You know when you've just been crying, and you wipe them away, and get into the mindset not to cry? But, as soon as you see someone, and they ask you if you're OK, and then all the tears come flooding back? Almost like a trigger that sets everything off? I know how Zara felt trying to make it look like she just had hay fever with puffy eyes and a snotty nose.

We packed, showered, and dressed into comfy joggers and baggy jumpers. We said our goodbyes to the family and said we would meet up soon, or every so often depending on my new and wilder schedule.

We jumped into the three black Range Rovers and headed to the airport with Jasmine and Jaimie. I was in the last car with Dean and Zara. I obviously sat in the middle because it was a little awkward between them.

As we approached the gates to the planes, I placed my large sunglasses on my head so I would be ready to look 'OK' for paparazzi in the airport windows. As the car stopped, I got out and swung my bag over my shoulder, I helped Dean gather his things and asked Pasher to take a photo of us outside the jet. Somehow, we managed to overtake the first car, so my dad and sister were still on their way, but the bodyguards and Pasher were here.

Dean and I posed for the camera and took our luggage on board. The plane was so neat and luxurious I immediately got excited, they even brought out a snack tray, with cakes and fruit as a treat. Zara ordered that in preparation.

There were two seats opposite each other, so I sat opposite Dean right at the back; we had our own area. As I heard more voices outside, I got off the plane to greet the others. They had a different plane to us, they were going back to Wales and we were going back home to Thailand; the others needed to get back quickly because of their priorities. I gave them both a huge hug and best wishes for their travel. I said I would see them at Jasmine's wedding.

We waved goodbye as they got on, and Zara as a present paid for their jet. We stayed a bit longer because Zara was a bit nervous for the plane ride, so Chris got her some drinking tea to calm her nerves.

We sat at the steps of the plane whilst Pasher and Jake were preparing everything on the jet. Dean and Zara made up and apologised to each other, so it took a lot weight off my shoulders.

Since I was bored, I ran over to the glass window that separated me from the paparazzi like a shield, and I did some poses for them. They were very happy, but then when everyone was ready to go, I blew some kisses to the people the other side of the window and sprinted to the plane and we all got buckled up.

We took off smoothly, and as we were in the air, I walked to freshen up in the bathroom, when a conversation started about where Dean was going to stay. I was confused because his mum lived near so there wasn't a problem.

I came back out and sat with a blanket wrapped around me (because it was cold with the air conditioning).

"So, what was that conversation about?" Everyone looked confused. I took a sip of my water and sat back. "Oh, come on, I heard you. Dean needs a place to stay. He can stay with us, but his mum lives near, is she away or something?" I took a bite of a strawberry.

"I snuck out," he admitted.

"What? Coming here?" I asked.

"Yeah, she never knew I left. So, she's going to kill me when she sees me. I just need to stay at yours for a night so I can think of a plan." He laid back in his chair and gazed out the small window.

"Oh." I placed my headphones on and listened to some old 80s pop music to cheer me up and take the awkward feeling away.

CHAPTER 30

We had an hour left of the journey, so I had to freshen up, again, to be ready for pictures. There was some crust arriving in my eye, after my long nap.

As I walked out to go to the bathroom, Dean got up after me and followed into the other sitting room (it was the only way to get to the bathroom, it was a long plane, but I'm not complaining).

"Hey, I didn't mean to end things so weirdly, I was too distracted with nervous feelings," he called down the aisle after me. I turned around and walked back to him, slowly.

"It's OK. Just ignore me next—" Before I finished speaking, he kissed my lips. I felt that time had stopped. I couldn't believe what was happening.

"I love you, Nova." He smiled and glared into my eyes. I got nervous and looked at the ground. He placed my hair behind my ear and strolled back to his seat, leaving me there lost for words. I smiled to myself and skipped to the bathroom, re-living the memory.

I showered, shaved my legs and curled my hair. Yes, I know showering twice a day is bad for you, but I just had to pass time. Don't suggest sleeping, I just can't sleep on a moving object. I brought a sneaky extra outfit with me, it was a pastel blue crop top, white long skirt (that flew in the wind) and pastel blue platforms. I still had my oversized glasses and white cap.

I walked down the aisle like a model, twirling around like a movie star. With no one in sight, it did feel magical because I was in a plane too. It almost felt like a movie, but my life was the movie, that's why I still couldn't believe it.

Then I rushed back to my seat, after we had some turbulence.

Everyone was amazed at my new outfit, well, basically jealous that they didn't bring a spare one for themselves. I then sat down and read some of my book, and after five minutes, I saw Dean staring at me with his gorgeous caramel eyes. I couldn't resist so I jumped over to sit on his lap and cuddle, his smile when I did lit me up, then we just stayed like that for the rest of the time, whilst I read and he played with my hair. It was the best feeling.

So, the journey took a bit longer than expected; there was a storm and we had to go around it. I had a lot of extra time. But, as time went by I amazingly did end up falling asleep on Dean's lap and after an hour, he woke me up ready to land.

As we hit the ground, and the plane bounced, I could see that the airport was flooded with people. I glanced through the humongous windows drowned with colours of clothes and flashing lights. Here we go again. At least I was in a good mood with everyone, so I wouldn't be so annoyed at the paparazzi all in my face making me have another breathing issue with panic and making a fool of myself in front of Dean.

We gathered our belongings and headed down the steps. Then I remembered that we didn't have to walk through the airport because the car was waiting outside the plane, so I held Dean's hand walked to the car with everyone else following.

Zara ordered a minibus to take us home, but it was a luxurious minibus (of course, Zara would never ride in anything other than superior), so as we stepped inside, the seats were in twos opposite each other, and there were four of them. So, Dean and I sat on the back ones, Zara and Pasher sat in the seats behind us at the front, and Chris and Jake sat on the ones opposite them.

I sat down and turned my 'aeroplane' mode off and hundreds of thousands of people started following me on Instagram. This is because from the flight to the other side of Australia I kept my phone on 'aeroplane' mode to keep Zara from reaching me; also that night was when Zara told the world about me. How wonderful.

"Ugh, Dean?" I said in concern. I turned my phone around so he could see what I'd been staring at for the last thirty seconds.

"Oh my gosh!" he squealed. "You're an Instagram star!" he yelled at the top of his lungs. Then everyone on the bus turned around and stared at me. Zara looked even more concerned.

"What?" She unbuckled her seatbelt and sat to the left of me. "What do you mean 'you're an Instagram star', Dean?" she panicked.

Dean grabbed the phone off me and shoved it in Zara's sight. "Look at how many followers she has gained overnight." I didn't think Dean knew the problem.

"No. This can't be right. I haven't said anything about you!" she shrieked. She looked at me as if I had said something. "Have you?"

"Are you serious?" I stared at her. "Remember the night you won your award, the same night I flew to Australia without your permission, and an interviewer asked you, "Would you like to have some kids one day?" I clapped my hands together. "Ring any bells, gossiper?" The look on Zara's face when she remembered. It looked as if she just killed someone.

Pasher came into the conversation. "I think you didn't remember because you got wasted with a few other celebs," he announced, trying to be the 'smart' one.

"I know, Pasher, you don't need to remind me," she quietly said, rubbing her forehead. "Are you OK with being in the spotlight this bad?" She looked up with her forehead wrinkles wrinkled.

"Well it isn't anything new. I have been in the spotlight ever since I met you. They knew I was your daughter; I just didn't think the world would find out so fast. You must be extremely famous for me to be found out that easily." I sat back. "But, it isn't your fault, Mum. It's just how the world works. They were going to find out about me anyway, it just came too quick for you to prepare me." I reached over and gave her a hug; she looked stressed, and extremely tired with a vein right down her forehead.

As she walked back to her seat, the driver set off and we were heading back home, after what seemed like an eternity since we'd been here last.

We drove down the driveway and a lady was standing outside the door. Since I couldn't see her properly, I thought it was Dean's mother, so I panicked and told Dean to duck, but as we got closer and closer, Zara announced, "She's here!" Excitedly. As you could tell everyone was bewildered. This was not his mother.

We stopped right next to the front door, and as soon as the doors flung open Zara leapt out to greet this stranger in my eyes. I got up and pulled Dean with me. (I was going to go and collect my stuff afterwards, but Pasher was carrying it in for us, he was such a gentleman.)

"Nova, I want you to meet your new..." She paused.

"Assistant!" Belle eagerly revealed. "Hi I'm Belle. B E L L E. You really are gorgeous." She jumped forward and hugged me 'til I literally could not breathe. I patted her on the back.

"Wow. I really don't know what to say. Well, firstly, hi, I'm Nova. N O V A, and thanks." I crossed my arms and turned angrily to Zara who looked really happy. "Mum, could I talk to you outside for a second?" I pivoted to Dean and whispered to take Belle into my room to show her around, and then I smiled at this new person in my life. As they strolled on inside with the guards and Pasher following, I vigorously turned to Zara.

"When I said I want to be independent here and that I don't want anything from you that would make me dependant on you and money, this isn't what I had in mind."

"I got you an assistant to help you with your singing career. I thought she could do some confidence activities with you and help plan things for you. She can help." She crossed her arms.

"That, I'm fine with, but I know that's not the only reason. You want to make me dependant on her. Make her do everything for me. If I do ever want to go forward with my singing career, I want to do the majority by myself, the majority of it is getting into the right lifestyle, confidence she can help with, everything else I want to challenge myself on my own. I will ask you for help, but no complete stranger that spells out her name to people when she first meets them," I argued.

"She's a very sweet girl that wants to make you happy, she's here to help. I'm glad you want to challenge yourself, but when it comes to big careers like this, you'll need help and I'll be too busy with my own career. I will be here to support you all the way, but not to book your whole schedule. Give her a chance, this can really help. Whenever it comes to anything as big as a business, actress, or especially singers, everyone will always have help, no matter how big the problem, the people that are there to help can make that problem micro small and they'll be there to help you the whole way. They're here to make things easier, not harder." She rubbed my shoulder.

We sat on the bench nearby and she carried on. "When I wanted to become an actress, I wanted to get there all by myself with no help, I was just like you. I dreamed of saying, 'Oh yeah I got here all by myself,' because that would allow me to sleep at night, to be able to say to myself that I had earned this because I did it all by myself. But, when I started practicing for auditions, it was so hard emotionally, because I put way too much pressure on myself, if I didn't act good enough or if I couldn't cry on cue. I would cry to my parents just before bed, but I never told them the stress I felt. It messed with my schoolwork because I could never concentrate. One night, I just let it out to my dad and he gave me the most amazing, heartfelt speech about how everyone needs help; even if you are just building a shed, you would need someone to hold up the wall, so you could nail it in place. But a challenge this big, is too big to be taken on by itself." I started to cry and dig my head into her shoulder to dry the tears. I really felt this. I knew she was right. But, I didn't want to believe it because, it was true, I wanted to get there all by myself.

"So, do you promise to let me get you help?" I nodded, melting under pressure. "Look, I know you can do this, but I don't want you feeling the way I did, it's natural to feel upset and depressed at times because not everything goes our way. But I look at it that, it's a sign that there's something much greater we can do. I'm not saying be positive all the time, you have to let your emotions flow freely at some point or you'll burst!" I laughed. "But, don't take everything to heart, baby." I sat up and gave her the biggest hug.

"I love you. You really are my hero." She kissed my cheek and dried my tears with her sleeve, and we shook it off and walked positively and with a new mindset, into the house.

"Belle!" I shouted into the echoed hallways. All of a sudden, she shot down the stairs and ran to me like she needed help. She stood upright and curtsied. "No need for that. I want to be your friend, I don't want you thinking you have to work for me, I want you to think of it as my emotional support and friend that books my schedule, nothing more workwise. We can celebrate together, go through hard times and good, and rule the world together." She smiled so hard; you would never believe. She opened her arms wide and I jumped into them like a monkey and laughed all the way through it.

Pasher ordered some Indian takeaway and it showed up shortly after. We all sat in the colossal lounge and watched Netflix until we fell asleep. As my eyes were closing, I woke up Dean and took him with me to wash our faces because I was so tired.

Obviously, to ruin the moment, I got soap in my eye so that really woke me up, but then I settled down in bed and Dean slept on the floor on an air mattress. He kissed my cheek goodnight and then we slept for hours.

The next morning, Belle came in all dressed, fresh face with a tray full of patisseries and cups of tea to freshen the palette. Dean slept a little while longer and after I finished, I hopped in the shower to get ready to meet face to face with what seemed like an angry mother; it was time to see Dean's mum. I know I shouldn't shower this much because it's bad for the natural hair oil, but I was really dirty from the Indian food stuck on my legs from last night (trust me I don't know how it got there).

I came out and did my proper facial routine (I literally got a bar of soap and shoved it in my eye last night because I was so tired). I dried my hair and since it's naturally straight, all I did was put it in a high ponytail. I walked out and Dean was awake laying on the bed up against the headboard staring at the ceiling, so I pushed him into the bathroom and told him to have a shower. He was even messier than me, believe it or not. He had chicken in his ear, along with crusty sauce under his fingernails. What did we do last night, seriously?

I wandered into my wardrobe and chose a pink denim dungaree

with a white crop top underneath. I put on white platforms and bounced on my bed and checked Instagram to see how many followers I had gained. Not going to lie, I felt pressured to post, but I thought I would leave it until I was ready. I placed on my headphones and jammed to some music whilst I waited for Dean.

Half an hour later, he came out clean with curly hair; he brought an outfit and some shampoo with body wash with him to Australia, only when he thought we were staying there for a while.

As we were both ready, we headed downstairs to find waffles with Nutella on the table (even though we just had patisseries, we couldn't resist). So, we sat down and enjoyed our meal. Shortly after, Zara came in and announced that the car was waiting outside, it was four of us going including Chris the bodyguard, but he was also the driver of the Range Rover and protection in case a fight broke out.

We got in and Zara sat in the front to lead the way. I held Dean's hand, well, squeezed it, all the way because he was shaking with fear. I thought his mum would understand, but he was acting like she would kill him. I kept reminding him that we would all keep him safe, but he kept worrying. I couldn't blame him.

As we pulled up, police were at her house. So, Dean and I stayed put in the car whilst Zara and Chris went to investigate. "Hi. What's going on?" Zara 'casually' strolled on over.

"You wouldn't have known where he'd gone, would you?" Billie screamed as she ran to Zara. "He just disappeared. In the night too." She looked as if she'd been up all night by the way she was rubbing her eyes and forehead. Well, what parent wouldn't be?

Zara slowly told Billie where he was. Meanwhile back in the car, Dean said something depressing that emphasised how frightened he was.

"She's going to kill me. I should just run away now; we should've never come here." I leant over and gave him a hug and a kiss on the shoulder.

"Everything will be fine because you have us to protect you. You are family to us, nothing less." I tried to calm him down.

Then all of a sudden, Billie started banging on the car window of Dean's seat and was yelling, "GET OUT!" ferociously. She looked like a zombie.

Dean whimpered and jumped over to my side. I found some pepper spray in the door compartment to protect us; I guess that was for Zara against threat. I guarded Dean with my body and the spray, but Dean wanted to protect me, so he climbed in front and held my hand from behind. She managed to smash the window and reach her hand far into the back seat. (You would be thinking at this point since the police were there, they would've heard and would be rushing to the rescue, but apparently not.)

What I didn't know was that Zara was pushed over the wall and rolled down the hill by Billie in rage, and Chris was sprinting after her, that's why I was also confused that Chris wasn't coming to protect us, but what he did do before was that he locked the car, so we'd be safer.

Anyway, as Billie got in, I waited for the moment for her eyes to be vulnerable so I could shoot. I didn't get the chance because she was jumping around like a monkey, which led to her knocking it out of my hand. (Yes, at this point half her body was in the car, and I was screaming as Dean was trying to push her out.) As she stopped, she looked me in the eye from behind Dean.

I slowly moved in front of Dean because I thought she had a weapon and I didn't want him to get hurt. Dean tried to push me back, but I was resilient.

"Move!" I stayed put for Dean's sake. "I said move!" I hated this.

I really hated this.

"Mum, what do you want?" Dean said mercifully. "Just calm down!" Oh no, you should never say that to an angry person.

"Calm down!?" She breathed very deeply. "How can I CALM DOWN when you're missing?! So, you just think it's OK for you to get on a PRIVATE jet and fly to AUSTRALIA?! And you think I would be calm?! Think, you idiot, does that seem right?!" She grabbed his arm that protected me around the waist and, not going to lie, it did feel like a punch to the stomach. I held in my moan to not make it seem like she was winning.

Then I grabbed her arm, oh she looked me deeply in the eye. I felt like she was sucking my soul out through my throat. She really had the death stare all sorted. I slowly let go and surrendered.

"Look, we can give you anything, anything you want, just don't hurt him," I pleaded. Thinking back, I did sound weak and defenceless, but I think if you were trying to protect your crush and the person who made you feel special from their aggressive mother, you would be pretty frightened too. I mean, if Dean was scared of his own mother, there's no reason for me to be OK with her, he's the only one who really knows her. If it were a complete stranger, I would have sprayed the pepper already, but this was Dean's mum and I didn't want to put her through any pain.

She backed up because she acknowledged our petrified faces. "I just want to talk to you, Dean." She stood there waiting for an answer with her hands gripping the smashed windowpane frame. There was no answer for a while; she got frustrated. "DEAN! GET OUT! I just want to talk to you before I lose my patience and hurt someone." OK, firstly, she already lost her patience and secondly, she's already hurt everyone here, maybe not all physically, but definitely emotionally.

I moved into the middle seat a bit more at rest. Dean rushed to climb out of the window, but he pulled me with him to keep him calm. Billie told me to go and see Zara, but I looked at Dean to check it was OK.

"Yeah, you can go. Just come back, OK?" He anxiously grabbed my arm in terror.

I ran to the bottom of the hill to find Zara lying on the floor with her hand on her back. "Oh my gosh!" I combed my fingers through my hair anxiously. "Mum?!" I fell to the ground, placed my hand on her head, and held her hand. Chris called the ambulance because the police that were here told them to. We did have a first aid policewoman with us, but the rest were with Billie and Dean; there was only three of them altogether. I sat with her in the back and kept reassuring her. Dean knew I was in the ambulance, so he left and got a taxi after us.

As we arrived at the hospital, they rushed us in quickly because they were extremely busy. We were put in a private, quiet room where the nurses checked on her. I was told to leave the room because the injuries were dreadful, so I met Dean out the front. It turned gloomy outside and windy, but it was light and warm in the waiting room with windows looking out. But the best thing was, there were no paparazzi.

"Is she OK?" He ran to me, worried. I hugged him instantly and he swung me around. If you need to imagine it, it was like we were reuniting for the first time in years. It was emotional because I hate seeing my family injured.

"Yeah, she'll be fine. They said it was her back, she said as she rolled down the hill, she smashed over a pointy rock and it caught her right in the bone," I weakly said. Dean wanted to make me feel better, so he took me to the hospital café, and we sat in the sofa chairs. Super comfy. I never would have thought that a quiet hospital café would be romantic, but Dean just made everything romantic.

We sat by the window on the sofas and ordered some doughnuts and mochas. "So, what do you want to talk about?" He took a bite of the glazed doughnut. I shrugged, still a bit unhappy.

"I'm not sure. What's on your mind?" I sat back, sipping my warm drink.

"Well, I was thinking, if Zara is OK and we get out of here sooner than later, I was wondering, just me and you go somewhere. Because we've only had a couple of dates and they both got ruined." He took a gulp of his drink.

"Sure, where do you want to go?" I took a bite of my food, feeling a bit happier.

"Movies then restaurant!" he excitedly said. "I have thought about this for so long, I have even dreamt about it, I think it will be so romantic and it will take a lot of misery off our minds." He smiled.

"Wow, I love it. It sounds perfect. But, there's one thing. Paparazzi," I pouted.

"Well, they have seen me before at the airport so there's nothing new. Let's give them something to talk about."

"OK, it's on. Tonight?" I felt so grown up.

"Yeah!" He sat up, reaching for my hand.

"How's your mum?" I asked because I left them in an argument.

"She doesn't ever want to see me again. She went on about saying that she can't afford to keep me, because she's in debt. She can't pay for me to go to school and for me to go out and meet up with friends because we have to save up and pay for bills and food. She said if I want to stay, I have to get a job and give her all the money." He placed his head in his hand and sulked. I moved over to sit next to him and give him a squeeze and embrace.

"You don't deserve this; I will promise to always look after you." I wiped his tears that streamed down his face.

"Thank you, I really don't deserve you," he cried.

"You can live with us, you can be home schooled with me and we can go to Zara's set, we can tour the world and adopt puppies." We laughed. "You'll be so much happier."

So, we finished up with food and slept on the sofas up until 9:30pm. Chris came to wake us up and took us into the Range Rover that was driven by another driver. I thought Zara was in the car, but as we jumped in, Chris shut the door and the driver sped off. It turns out that Zara needed to stay overnight because her back was in much pain. So, we just napped in the car and went straight to bed as we got in. Pasher was in the living room looking after us for the night. I slept in my bed and Dean was on an air mattress on the floor. Like last night.

CHAPTER 31

In the morning, Pasher let us sleep in because we were exhausted from the last week. At 12:30pm, Dean woke up and went in the shower (turns out we didn't go on our date last night, we fell asleep. Yes, I know it would have been too late to do it anyway, but we weren't aware of how late and how fast the day had gone). When the shower turned on it woke me up, so I picked my outfit for the date. I went in the shower after, and we both went downstairs in our outfits ready for breakfast. I chose my outfit to be matching colours with his that he brought – baby blue with white. I had white jeans with a baby blue blouse. We both had white trainer platforms on. Mine had a hint of baby blue around the lace.

For breakfast we ate in the make-up chairs and had a full English breakfast made by our chef. I had my hair put into a French braid with mascara and concealer to hide my dark circles from the sleep I'd missed. Dean had his hair in a quiff.

As we finished, our driver took us out in the limo with Chris and we headed to the city centre where we found the cinema. Paparazzi were everywhere, sorting their cameras out. Somehow Dean got excited, he really liked this life. The driver parked up and Chris got out and backed the people out of the way.

"You ready to be swarmed?" I smiled.

"As ready as I'll ever be. I just have to smile." He laughed. "I'll protect you."

"Thanks. Here we go." As I opened the door, the many voices toppled over each other, the sound of the camera clicks were like flies buzzing everywhere. We smiled and posed for a photo and ran into the building, laughing.

"That was so fun!" Dean shouted. We ran up the escalator and chose the movie and snacks. Chris was planning to wait outside in the seating area until our movie was finished, but he had been too nice for me not to get him a ticket, so I let him choose a film and we separated to go see our movies.

We sat right at the back; there was only another couple there, just like before. The film started and we relaxed, munching on our snacks. Nothing else happened after that, weirdly. Although, every time I went to hold Dean's hand, he went for popcorn instead. Did I do something? Maybe he just didn't see me? Am I overthinking? Am I overthinking about overthinking?

We exited the room and Chris's film had another hour, so we sat at the seating area and ate the last of our food.

I had a gulp of my drink and took a long swallow. "Is everything OK?" I asked, trying to sound casual.

He hesitated, "Nova, I have something to tell you." He paused again. "Something you're going to hate me for." He took a bite of his chocolate bar. Stalling.

I placed my hand on his knee. "I will never hate you. I mean, you've just gone through a lot so I wouldn't blame you for anything." I tried to give him a reassuring smile, but my lip quivered instead.

He took a deep thoughtful breath. "I never liked you like that, like loved you, I never felt it, I still can't feel it, I've tried but there's nothing there." He looked like he was guilty.

My heart had just been shot. My stomach flipped. Shivers ran up my legs. I immediately took my hand away from his knee and placed it on mine. The cold sweat came down my back. My arm hairs stood on end. I didn't say anything for a while. I had just been played; my relationship had been faked all this time? How?

"I'm sorry. I just couldn't go on," Dean whispered. With watery eyes.

He stood up and left the cinema. I just sat there in despair. Waiting for Chris to come out. I couldn't stop shaking with confusion and foolishness. I should have seen the signs, but I was new to this, so I didn't know what they were.

For a second, just a second, I actually thought that someone loved me for who I was. I had always been teased in school that no-one would ever love me. When will it ever be real for me? Will anyone ever love me?

A few moments later I fell on the floor and laid there (without a care in the world of what anyone thought of me), with food scattered all over my clothes, with oceans of tears ready to be released. Why is my life such a lie? Why is everything so beautiful ripped out of my life so viciously? I couldn't think straight. The noises around me felt like whispers in the wind; the lights dimmed as my eyes became cloudy from misery.

An old lady with four grandchildren was exiting the theatre, when she saw me suffering on the ground like a shrivelled-up fish gasping for water (if that helps your imagination of the scene). She told her grandchildren to go and watch the trailers on the walls whilst she came over to see if I was still alive. "Are you alright, dear?" She leant over, covering the bright ceiling light from my vision.

I nodded with small movements, staring at the same spot on the ceiling. She put down her bag and help lift me from the floor. I sat on the chair and cried. "My life is awful! Everything good that happens gets ruined somehow."

"Oh, honey. I'm sure everything will get better. Tell me what happened." She held my hand.

"My...... my...... boyfriend just broke up with me." I sounded so cliché, but little did she know that every tragedy that has happened in the last couple of weeks had built up my emotions even more, but this, it hurt so much. "I don't even know if we were going out, because he said to me that he never liked me in the first place. I have just been played and used and mocked by the person who I thought really liked me." I wiped my tears with my pinkie finger.

"You know some people are so jealous of others because they're so happy, that they just want to show them pain, to give an example of what maybe they've gone through. If he was never in the first place, then it's a sign that he was definitely not the person you should be lovin'. Find someone that loves you more than you love them because then you know for sure it'll last," she demanded. She was very headstrong; she knew her stuff. I was happy that she found me.

"But how will I know it's real?" I overthought.

"They'll tell you they love you at random times all throughout the day, every day. They'll always want to be with you, they'll stand by every decision you make. They'll always want to cuddle and make you laugh. It will be obvious. When you know you know, it's a feeling that will be so strong. Let's just say it'll be different from what you've just gone through. Much different."

"But I thought I knew with Dean." I couldn't stop, I was so interested in what she could teach me.

"Well you thought you did, but when a new person comes and they give you all the signs and don't hold back, you'll see the difference between fake and real love. Even though love at this age is rare, it can still happen. But, let love find you, don't go searching, your time will come. Everyone's will." She stood up, combed my hair behind my ear and walked off shouting the names of her grandchildren.

I sat there in disbelief of how right this lady was. I'm not going to waste my time over a stupid boy. I felt so much better, but I still wanted to know why Dean even went out with me.

I sat there scanning social media for whether anything had been leaked about the relationship (only because paparazzi were outside, and they saw him walk in with me). Nothing. Well, not yet. I texted Zara to see if she was any better. She replied soon after saying she was on her way to the cinema. I was confused because we were meeting her back at the house, but it's better this way.

Suddenly, Chris came out from behind the corner with his rubbish and walked over. "Where's Dean?" He sat down opposite. The tears started to flood back to the rim of my eyes. I blinked and they all came flooding out. "What's happened?" He rose his eyebrow.

"He never liked me," I whined, wiping my tears again. "He said he never did. I just feel that I've been used. Is there something I should've known that you know?" I looked at him intensely, with a snotty nose. He looked concerned, like I found out something that he already knew, that I wasn't supposed to find out.

"Ugh, yeah. There's something. Do you want to go and get food and talk about it then?" He always knew what I needed, but I just had to find it out first, then food.

"No. I want to know. Food after," I ordered.

He sat down and texted someone on his phone (later on I found out that he texted Zara to check if it was OK to tell me, but he just told me before she texted back). He placed his phone in his inside pocket and looked as if he was going to tell me something very important. To me it was. He was extremely professional and serious.

"Nova, what I tell you now, you can't hate Zara. She thought about this very hard and for a very long time, just think about what I'm saying. It will not be as it seems, OK?" He crinkled his forehead, placing his hands together on his knee. I nodded. "Zara thought it was best if you broke up." My mouth dropped to the floor, but I didn't speak because I listened to what Chris said before. He carried on, "She thought that Dean was going to hold you back from your dreams of singing, so she talked to Dean and he agreed to break up. Everything he said wasn't true, because he did really like you. Dean needed to make it seem real enough for you to believe it." He paused. "You can talk now."

"I don't know what to say. If he really liked me, why would he do this? Where is he going to stay? He would never hold me back from my dream. I don't understand, if I liked someone, surely Zara would understand not to get in the way. I mean I still like him, why would she break something so precious to me?" I questioned, suspiciously.

"Zara paid Dean." I slapped my hand on my forehead so hard I almost forgot everything he just said.

"WHAT?! How much?" I yelled.

"£25,000," he whispered.

"I can't hear you." I leaned forward.

"£25,000, Nova." He spoke louder.

"I'm not even surprised. Of course, she would. She's absolutely absurd, pathetic and jealous." I ground my teeth. "Let's get food and get home!" I stood up and headed for the escalators. Chris followed behind quickly, worried. Paparazzi were flooding the pavements, and I was hearing questions I didn't want to hear.

"What happened with that boy, Nova?" a man shouted and others followed. I stood there and stared at the cameras.

"My mother happened." I shoved them out of the way. (I would never intentionally hurt someone like that, but a demon broke through my soul that I couldn't control.) I stormed into the car.

We went through a drive through and got burgers and ice cream. Then we raced home to deal with this stupid situation. Chris told Zara to meet us at home because I was angry. Really angry.

We approached the drive and I swung open my door while the driver was still moving. He stopped immediately and I sprinted to the front door and knocked it so forcefully it echoed in the house. Zara came to the window and the expression on her face looked as if she killed someone, again, so guilty. She knew what was up. I had completely forgot that she had just damaged her back because she had damaged my soul.

She slowly opened the door and I pushed it so firmly it hit the wall behind, and she flew a few footsteps back. "Who do you think you are?" she yelled at me.

"Get in the lounge and sit!" I screamed back at her. Chris was behind me, ready to break up a fight. We stormed into the seating area and sat far away from each other. "Why did you do that? Pay Dean to break up with me. That was my boyfriend, Mum, I had something with him. He made me so happy and feel so special that you just had to take that away from me. You think that he was going to keep me from my dream? You psychopath. Was the real reason because you were jealous?"

"I know what I'm doing, I know if they're trouble or not, he was trouble about to happen. When I was in the hospital, while you were with him, I got a call from the police, saying his mother had been arrested. Dean didn't know that before I texted him, before you went on your date today. He has been taken to an orphanage and is staying there for a while. I also looked at his personal record that the police gave to me, it had theft written all over it. I didn't know this, but know I do and I'm keeping you as far away from him as I can. That's why his mother is poor, from all the things Dean had stolen that she had to pay for. There were things like diamond earrings and gold watches, all adding up into the hundreds of thousands. Now he's put his mother in jail because of the stress he put her through. That's why I did what I did." She pouted her lips and crossed her legs. "So, don't you come yelling at me, when you don't know the full story."

"What?" I really was lost for words. "Then why did you pay him to leave me?" I scratched my arm. "Why couldn't you just tell him to leave?"

"Because I felt bad that he had a bad start to life, so when he moves out, he can have a head start." She rubbed her hands together.

"Well, thank you for looking out for me. It was nice what you did. I knew you wouldn't do it to break something I enjoyed. Or I hoped anyway." I walked over and gave her a squeeze.

"Anything for you, sweetie. I know you didn't like me getting you things so I thought I would protect you double as much instead, even though I couldn't protect you any more than what I was already doing." She kissed my forehead. Then we binged watched Netflix and ate loads of chocolate and grapes. Random combination, I know, but delicious.

As Zara's house cleaners were here, we asked them to bring down three mattresses so we could sleep in the lounge. We invited Pasher over and bought loads of clothes online and ordered Chinese food to snack on. We went to bed quite early because all of us were exhausted. That was our night.

In early sunrise, as dusk settled and birds fluttered from the trees, I got up, placed on my workout clothes and went to our gym room and ran for a while to clear my head. I was surprised to see Zara join me ten minutes into the run. Then we placed ourselves onto the bikes and talked about my future.

"I'm all about moving fast in this industry, so is there anything you would love to do in the next couple of months?" Zara wanted to help me get out there. I thought long and hard every time before I went to bed if I wanted to do anything, I did. I had an idea.

"Yeah, I want to help people," I said proudly.

"That's lovely. How would you want to do that?"

"Well, I was thinking of making a video, a long video, interviewing people, including you and just being inspirational." I smiled.

"That's amazing, well I'll talk to Belle and we can get that started. We'll get a building to film it in, a camera crew, do you want random people?"

"Yeah, as many random people as you can, all different people, even homeless people, old, young, black, white, Asian, British, American, Australian, all over the world, we'll fly them here and start the interviews." I got excited.

"Wow, are you going to make questions?"

"Yes, I'll do the speaking and host the whole event." That was that. Final. I was going to finally make a difference in this world. What I had promised God this whole time. (I was going to do more as well, hopefully without the help of Zara and money, just on my own.)

As we exited the gym, we had showers, breakfast, and I had my first meeting on the dinner table with Belle, Zara's assistant (Shelly), Pasha and another assistant to be sending the promotion of the event. It went really well. As we finished up Zara and I visited the place where the filming was going to be; it was huge and unnecessary, but I felt so powerful and content, that I was really going to help these people feel special and important.

We returned home and enjoyed some food and headed to bed – it was a very quick day.

Fast forward a couple weeks (recap: all that we did was plan and set up the event with more people applying every day). It was the first day of filming and I had my little make-up on and silk red dress on, with nude heels and a space bun for the hairstyle. Everything was set up when we arrived at 8 o'clock in the morning. I had my flash cards with questions and quotes and I made up and some funny jokes if needed to brighten the mood because these were going to be deep questions.

I sat in my chair, Pasher touched up my hair and the cameras were rolling. I talked to the camera to introduce the film and behind the camera crew was a line of people quietly talking, about their interviews about to happen.

So, I started talking. "Hi. Some of you might know me to be Zara Whittle's daughter. I am and my name is Nova Whittle. It has only been a couple of months into this new lifestyle, after I found out who my real mother was. I have had a very traumatic life, but Zara has really taught me to be myself and to use these painful experiences to my advantage. So, I have decided to make this film all about self-confidence and to help people all over the world, in troubled scenarios and just in general with mental health. I will be talking to people all over the world about their lives and I will be giving advice from the lessons I have learned over time. Use all of the information from everyone to help you through your own problems." The introduction was over and I had not yet broken a sweat, and then the first person came in, a lovely dressed black woman from Holland, she was so kind and friendly and really opened up about her mistakes she made and how she helped others through their problems.

"When I started getting bullied in school, it really started me off on the wrong foot about life and that everything was going to be bad.

My mother and father left me as a child so I was adopted into a very strict household and I could never enjoy myself with fun teenager things like the cinema or parties, I had to study and I basically spent ninety percent of my life locked in my room. It was depressing and the bullying never got any better, so for my 16th birthday, I asked for a therapist. My mother actually let me get one, so I had three sessions and they went really well and my advice that I got was, whatever others think of me was never any of my business, which meant that I should stop thinking too much and that I never needed to know what those bullies thought of me, because anything they said was nonsense because they didn't know what was happening in my life and were pretty stupid, y'know, they just went on and on about rubbish, but in the end I just laughed because I turned out having better grades, I had turned out prettier than them, as everyone told me, and I now have my own family who show me how lucky and special I am every day. Family is everything and they just make me laugh every time I see them, so I am grateful that my parents were strict because I wouldn't have gotten to where I am today. I believe that everything happens for a great reason. Those bullies made me stronger, so I wouldn't change my childhood for a single second. Even though it was tough, it was so worth it."

She was really strong with her story and taught me about the true meaning of understanding that bullies are bullies because they are so jealous of you, because they want what you have. They bully because they want to give other people pain that they've gone through to show them how they've actually felt in the past. The best advice she gave was to laugh and ignore, making them feel bored of themselves.

Next, we had a British man, he was quite shy but gave his all.

"I was in a plane crash when I was a teenager. I was flying on my own to visit a family member. As we were descending pretty fast, I was petrified for my life. I had to hold a stranger's hand, because I could barely breathe. So we landed in the ocean and the inflatables inflated, but the impact was awful. We were in the ocean for a while and soon a ship passed and picked us all out of the ocean. We did have people that died on that flight, but I was super lucky. I just felt my guardian angel with me the whole time. From that experience I have taken that, your life can change within a matter of seconds, so take every chance you can in life and if it isn't worth it, you can still say that you've tried and you will progress if you just take any opportunity because anything can happen." I think I needed this advice a while ago. But he was awesome and got braver throughout the interview.

Then, we had twenty more people interviewed over the next couple of days (I narrowed it down otherwise the film would be six hours long).

As I had to finish the film, I brought in Zara to help with the summary of all of the influential information.

We sat together on the sofa in front of the camera and started rolling, again. "Wow, that was amazing advice from all of these very inspirational and strong people. Whatever you're going through, there is always light at the end of the tunnel. No matter how hard or difficult, there are people to help, people in the same situation, even family can give the best advice to comfort you. If you don't have family, go to friends or therapists or even teachers, they can help too," I added.

"Yeah, never give up on your dreams. There will be hurdles, there will be mistakes and mental breakdowns, you most likely will get to your tipping point, but I promise there's a solution and a better option for everything. If you need motivation, push yourself because no-one's going to do it for you, they'll have their own problems. If you need help because you're depressed or weak with the thought of failure, if you try but fail and still go on, you're not just a fighter to keep going you're also a warrior to be able to find new ways around problems. Love yourself and have confidence in your unique ways, ignore and block out the negative people and thoughts and walk by them like they're a rubbish bin full of banana peels." We both laughed.

"You're beautiful, handsome and courageous, everybody should be told that, if you haven't yet, let us be the first. Keep striving for your dreams. All of your insecurities are your unique features; embrace them and give them power, because that's the strongest thing you could do for yourself. Use your hobbies to your advantage, things you love and enjoy will be easy to pass time and make you happier. If you really have hit rock bottom, the best thing is to cry because the strongest people let their emotions fly free. Weak people keep them bottled inside for other people not to see." I had so much to say.

"Help others and remember that there is always hope for a better future if you make the small powerful changes to your mindset."

"We hope you have felt more at ease with knowing that there are so many people out there just like you, and that you can be just as happy as us now that we have learned from our mistakes. We love you and want to help more and more people, so visit our website and feel free to contact our employees for help." I had finished.

"Keep striving for the better," Zara ended, we both smiled at the camera, and scene.

I had a warm, cosy feeling inside of me. I hope this video will help so many people. We went into the back room where everyone who we interviewed was; they were eating cake and drinking tea. We both thanked them and headed home after a long day. I placed my PJs on, and Zara and I sat on the couch and had a chat.

"I'm so proud of you," Zara announced. "I don't think many kids would have done what you did."

I gave her a hug. "I will carry on helping people. Next I want to travel to countries and meet poor families and have one-on-one chats." I took a bite of the chocolate cake on the coffee table, then we had a very peaceful night and celebrated a new and proper next chapter.

So, that was my life up until I was fifteen. I kept going with the motivational videos on Instagram, I visited families, I went to my sister's wedding that was delayed a couple of months later because Wales had bad weather, that's nothing new. I felt really good about myself, and so many people had reached out and had thanked Zara and myself.

From my life I had learned that, everything happens for a reason, even reasons that don't concern you. Maybe you wanted something to happen and when it didn't it was to save someone's life; always look at the positives. Mistakes are made, and problems occur but, friends and family or anyone out there that cares about people (there are a lot), are there to support along the way. There will be extremely great days with amazing accomplishments, but you haven't experienced life without the bad days; we need them to grow. Everything you achieve is a wonderful stepping stone, even the small little details, to a more brighter you and an amazing future. There is hope when it rains, to water plants. There is hope with a hole in a jacket, a new fashion trend. Make things improve even when they're destroyed. Create new ideas, to help this world become a better place, because I think that's what everyone needs right now. Have confidence and an innovative mindset to achieve the goals no-one else would be able to do. You were born for a reason, so complete your mission, and succeed in what you love.

You can do this, just believe.

ABOUT THE AUTHOR

Carensa Harris is a fifteen-year-old girl, currently in year 11 doing her GCSEs. Fiction writing is how she can place her imagination onto paper and create great stories for others to enjoy. She started writing this book when she was twelve years old in 2017, when one English lesson changed everything. Ever since, she has been working on this book to get it perfect, and her personal touch is when she adds little pieces of advice throughout the book to hopefully help someone. She hopes to inspire the young and older generations to go and chase their dreams no matter what their age.